THE 1879 ANGLO ZULU WAR

A POTTED HISTORY & WARGAME RULES

12th Edition

Mark MacDuff

Copyright © Mark MacDuff 2018

Mark MacDuff has asserted his right under the Copyright, Designs and Patents Act 1988 to be identified as the author of this work

No part of this text may be reproduced or redistributed without the written consent of the author.

~ ~ ~

CONTENTS

- Wargaming the Zulu War
- Historical Background to the War
- The Armies
- British Forces
- Zulu Forces
- Formations

    The War:
    - January 22nd Inyezane
    - January 22nd First battle of Holbane
    - January 22nd Isandlwana
    - January 22nd Rorke's Drift
    - March 12th Ntombe Drift
    - March 28th Second battle of Holbane
    - March 29th Khambula
    - April 2nd Gingindlovu
    - July 4th Ulundi

- The Wargame Rules
- Conclusion
- Bibliography

Wargaming the Zulu War

I started wargaming the Zulu War in the 1980's using MiniFigs 25mm figures, Miniature Figurines Production Ltd, based back then in Southampton, England. Nowadays there is a really good choice of figure options for the wargaming of the Zulu War with numerous scales to choose from as well. I have written these rules, using 2 sets of movement and fire, so that the rules can be played perfectly well with either 20mm, 25mm or 28mm scale figures. You can use either of the scales of movement and fire. Most probably the key determining factors for you will be what size wargaming table you have, how many figures you are using and how long you want the wargame to last.

These rules have been tested over many wargames. Invariably after most wargames I find something has been thrown up that invites a modification to the rules and there's always scope for fine tuning. Each time I find something that can be improved, I adjust or add to the rules and issue a new edition, so now we are on the 12th edition.

The first sixty-odd pages of the book is a potted history of the Zulu War. I've read more than twenty books on the Zulu War and there is now a wealth of stuff out there on YouTube. Plenty of facts but also, sadly, there's still quite a few inaccuracies washing around. There is a certain inevitability that new writers will refer to older books without going to bother of fact checking original source material. This does mean that sometimes inaccuracies get repeated and over time embedded in the story of the Zulu War.

The second half the book is devoted to the wargame rules. Scales, unit values, movement, terrain, firepower, morale, concealment, ammunition expenditure, command etc are covered. I have factored in the difference between Zulu regiments raised shortly before the war and those raised from further back. Some regiments fielded included men in the sixties or even seventies. Others comprised warriors under the age of twenty. Obviously, these moved and fought differently, and the rules reflect this. Also allowed for is certain qualities that distinguished particular British units; for example, The Naval Brigade.

Background

The beginnings of the Zulu empire can be traced back to 1816 when Shaka came to power as chief of a small clan. Shaka was a gifted natural leader and military strategist and from humble beginnings he quickly built a formidable fighting force imbued with an esprit de corps that made it vastly superior to its adversaries.

Initially the Zulu empire expanded rapidly but it was then forced to contract under pressure from Boer encroachment. By 1879 the Zulu nation was encircled to the south by the British Colony of Natal, to the north-west by the Boer Orange Free State and British administered Transvaal and to the north by the Swazi Kingdom and Portuguese East Africa.

The Zulu King Cetshwayo attempted a policy of keeping on friendly terms with the British in the hopes that they would protect Zululand from the Boers but the British Governor of the Cape, Sir Bartle Frere, believed that Zululand should be annexed by the British.

Frere set about provoking the Zulus into starting a war by issuing Cetshwayo a series of demands that were wholly unreasonable, not least the dismantling of the Zulu army. Cetshwayo was reluctant to go to war but had little alternative and his army, untried in war for over two decades was keen to prove its worth.

The British had conducted numerous "native" campaigns in Africa and elsewhere as the British Victorian Empire had expanded. There had been nine "Frontier Wars" in South Africa and the last against the Xhosa had provided experience for several British units and numerous officers, including Lord Chelmsford, who would go on to fight in the Zulu war, only a year later. However, Chelmsford, in perhaps imagining the Zulu would fight much like the Xhosa, was to find out that he had made a wrong assumption, with catastrophic consequences in the opening stages of the war.

The Zulu war, interestingly, was actually not even authorised by London and Frere, along with the commander of the British forces in South Africa, Chelmsford, reckoned that they could invade Zululand and defeat the Zulus before London even got wind of what they were up to.

The invasion of Zululand began on January 11th 1879 and on January 22nd the British suffered one of their worst defeats at the hands of a native army during Queen Victoria's reign. The shockwaves from this were to eventually lead to the collapse of Disraeli's government but in the interim Britain was forced to pour more troops and money into the Zulu campaign. What had been regarded as little more than a "shooting party" by the officers who were present at the outset of war, quickly turned into a major campaign, reported in graphic detail by the British press to the public back home and observed with equal curiosity by other nations.

The Zulu war for the wargamer provides a stunning contrast of adversaries: the British – a modern fighting force armed with the latest breech loading rifles and the Zulus fighting shoulder to shoulder armed with shields and spears in a manner akin to the Roman legions of two thousand years earlier.

THE ARMIES

In 1879 the first effects of the reforms that were to run through the British army in the second half of the Victorian era, were just beginning to be felt. Whilst notionally progress through the ranks was possible and applications to the officer ranks could be made by a man of any social background, at the time of the Zulu war nearly all commissioned officers purchased their commissions. Most exceptions to this were in the artillery and engineers.

The British army in 1879 was considered one of the best in the world and the officers and ranks were imbued with a sense of their own superiority. Discipline and training were high, and equipment had, by the standards of the day, been thoroughly modernised. The British army had, since 1838, never lost any colonial campaign upon which it had embarked. They had recently begun to use the powerful, breech loading Martini-Henry rifle and breech loading artillery had just come into play. The newly invented gatling gun had been acquired and rocket launchers, in use for many years, had been refined and whilst not reliably accurate were believed to be very good at scaring native enemies.

General Lord Chelmsford who commanded the British forces at the outset of the war demonstrated a confidence bordering on arrogance when undertaking the invasion of Zululand. During the first campaign the officers, especially in the central column, to which Chelmsford attached himself, were infected by his confidence and regarded the campaign as little more than a "jolly hunting party". However, after the disaster of Isandlwana and the chaos of Holbane, the Zulu enemy quickly assumed the epic proportions of an unseen monster. British nonchalance had turned to neurotic caution. The second invasion was conducted with in comparison to the first the utmost care and Chelmsford this time took no unnecessary chances.

The Zulu army in 1879 was a military machine that could trace its roots back to 1816. However, it had not in essence changed since then. After the founder of the Zulu nation Shaka was assassinated in 1828 there were three rulers including Cetshwayo who was King at the time of the 1879 war. After Shaka came Dingane, whose rule was beset by hostilities with the Boers and after him came Mpande in 1838. Mpande seemed peaceable but during his long reign numerous more regiments were created to strengthen the Zulu army and many of them during the period when his nephew Cetshwayo held considerable influence.

The British decided to involve themselves in the Zulu nations affairs and determined to back Cetshwayo's half-brother Mbuyazi, who they felt could be more controllable than Cetshwayo. Increasingly in the last years of Mpande's rule the British made their presence felt and they put their influence behind Mbuyazi, but it turned out that they had back the wrong horse. There was a brief power struggle, Cetshwayo massacred his opponents' followers and secured the throne.

The scene was set for an inevitable confrontation.

British Forces

The backbone of the British army that invaded Zulu was a number of battalions of regular infantry supplemented by detachments of Naval Brigade, some regular cavalry, volunteer cavalry units, native units and some artillery. Rocket launchers and gatling guns were also used, the latter for the very first time. The Zulu War was just about the last campaign where the British troops invariably wore red jackets and blue trousers. That said, one regiment's traditional uniform was dark green. Add to this the jaunty blue and white and wide brimmed straw hats of the Naval Brigade, the fluttering red and white pennons on the lances of the 17th Lancers and the exotic regalia of the Zulus and you have a spectacularly colourful pair of opposing armies for the battlefield of the wargamer.

Initially a large quantity of local native troops was also raised at short notice and these Natal Native Contingent units provided a quantity of men but proved at first a total liability because they were badly led, poorly trained and poorly equipped. Uniform was no more than a red rag tied around the head or an arm with the exception of the Natal Pioneers who got to wear white knee length canvas trousers, old British infantry five button serge jackets and blue pillbox caps.

During the first campaign the Natal Native Contingent received only one rifle per 10 men. In the second campaign the majority of the NNC were disbanded but those that remained, excepting such units as Wood's

Irregulars, were equipped with one rifle per man. There was also a greater effort to train and drill the troops and to uniform them. Hence during the second campaign NNC carry a higher point value.

Cavalry for Chelmsford was an issue; simply put he didn't have any regular cavalry, so he had to rely on local volunteer and militia units. These included the Frontier Light Horse, Baker's Horse, Schermbrucker's Horse, Raaf's Transvaal Rangers, Weatherley's Border Horse, The Natal Carbineers, The Buffalo Border Guard, Newcastle Mounted Rifles and Natal Mounted Police and more besides. Most of these units numbered between just thirty to fifty men apiece. The largest unit was perhaps the Frontier Light Horse, who fielded just over two hundred men at the unit's height.

To augment his cavalry there were some mounted native volunteers who often fought well and finally the British Mounted Infantry. These units were generally drawn from the odds and ends of the regular units, bandsmen and the like, anyone really, so long as they claimed some familiarity with horses and a basic ability to ride. Given that the units were hastily assembled, and leadership was a bit of a job lot, these units must carry a slightly lower point value to units of Regulars. These units were raised to provide scouting forces and they were not intended as front-rank units to the same extent as the regular companies, hence their reduced point value. However, they did carry rifles not carbines and fought, when they had to, dismounted as infantry. Contemporary photographs show Mounted Infantry armed with rifles, but some also show them armed with carbines. It appears that the majority used rifles.

All told, Chelmsford had a decent force and certainly it seemed sufficient to deal with the Zulu. His Achilles heel however was in his providing transport for his supplies and the agonisingly slow speed at which his advancing columns were to move. There were never enough wagons and oxen and even mules were brought across from America in an effort to help ease the transport issue. This however did nothing to deter the officers from using endless wagons to shift the furniture, wines, clothes and essential luxuries without which they could not possibly travel.

Ulundi, the Zulu capital, lay seventy-five miles from the border. A seasoned rider could cover the journey in a day or two. A Boer commando or a Zulu impi in two or three days. But Chelmsford knew that it would take two weeks at the minimum for his ponderous force, even if everything went seamlessly. But this was still without reckoning on the wagons needed to move the army's equipment. A British battalion could march lightly equipped with enough water and food for a day, if each man relied on what he carried on his back. After that there was no food, no water. If a battalion was to take its cooking equipment, then that amounted to nine tons of extra kit to carry. A battalion's reserve ammunition was another ton. Their tents another couple of tons and for each day they needed another ton of food and a ton or two of firewood. Once Chelmsford had totted up the numbers, he was left realising that he needed wagons to shift 1,500 tons of stuff in order to get his forces to Ulundi.

It took Chelmsford a long time to assemble the wagons, oxen and drivers that he needed, and it cost him a fortune and by the end of the campaign the War Office had exceeded its normal budget by £4 million. In today's terms, around £400 million.

Eventually though he was all set to invade. He had given the Zulu King an ultimatum and Cetshwayo had until the 11th January to comply but impatient to get started Colonel Wood launched his column into Zululand a day early. The war, which the British Government didn't know about and that the Zulus hadn't invited had begun.

Zulu Forces

Zulu regiments were identified by the shield colour and regimental "uniform" which comprised various combinations of cow tail loin cloths, monkey skin head dresses, leopard skin headbands, ostrich feathers, genet tails, crane feathers and so forth. Often in battle, but not always, much of this highly ornate uniform was discarded. For wargaming purposes, it adds enormous colour and makes it easy to distinguish between regiments.

The main Zulu weapon was the thrusting spear, alternatively called the assegai or iklwa. Throwing spears were also carried. Some warriors carried clubs – knobkerries. Muzzle loading muskets were in circulation but were eschewed by most Zulus. After the British defeat at Isandlwana the Zulus took possession of a thousand or more breech loading Martini-Henry rifles.

The Zulu shield was made of cow hide. Young regiments without battle honours carried black shields or brown shields. As battle honours were gained the shields were replaced with ones which mixed black with white or red with white. Veteran regiments carried all white shields. Most veteran, white shield regiments ranks were older men, whilst black shield regiments were made up of young men desperately keen to prove their valour.

The Zulu army in 1879 had not seen active service for 23 years. The Zulu King Cetshwayo had raised just three regiments since he had formerly come to the throne although he had been instrumental in raising regiments before this date. He pursued a policy of peaceful overtures towards his British neighbours. Nevertheless, whilst he adopted a policy of non-aggression towards his white neighbours, he certainly took steps to keep the Zulu military machine well-oiled and in 1879 the Zulu army was without doubt one of the best indigenous armies in the whole African continent.

The Zulu regimental system showed order, discipline and co-ordination. However, it was an army that had not modernised or changed for fifty-years, and it had refused to recognise or consider that disciplined ranks of thrusting-spear wielding warriors were no match when pitched against lines of trained soldiers with breech loading rifles supported by artillery, gatling guns and cavalry. In fairness to the Zulus though they had never experienced these before. Yes, they had fought the Boers, who were superb marksmen and yes they did possess rifles but these were invariably obsolete items sold to them by Portuguese traders and many were muskets and ammunition was often homemade and quite often nothing better than small round stones rammed down the unrifled barrels. The Zulus had no idea of what the firepower of disciplined ranks of British infantry meant. Their first real taste of this was Isandlwana and it is a testament to their courage that they faced it and overcame it, despite appalling casualties. The Zulu victory at Isandlwana showed the Zulu war machine was a force to be reckoned with and that raw courage in the face of highly destructive enemy modern rifle fire was, combined with discipline, a force of formidable power.

The Zulus did have a clear appreciation of the effectiveness of movement in skirmish order when facing heavy fire and the image, as portrayed in the film Zulu, of them being prepared to be cut down as they advanced in lines, is hardly accurate. At Isandlwana and elsewhere they skirmished with such precision that they received grudging admiration from their opponents and several British officers and war correspondents commented upon their skill at skirmishing. The Zulu army was well disciplined and had a battle plan that was invariably thought out before the battle and that all the regimental commanders were well briefed and knew exactly what they had to do.

The Zulu army had incredible esprit de corps and an unshakeable belief in their own superiority. Their modus operandi was simple: find the enemy, encircle them, destroy them. Their grasp of tactics was sound and their strategy, whilst perhaps not subtle, was certainly objective and reasoned.

When the British invaded Zululand in three columns the Zulu response was to send two smaller impis against the British flanking columns to pin them down or at least harass them and to unleash their main impi against the British central column. They recognised that having destroyed the British centre column, the flanking columns would, at a stroke, be isolated from each other and could then each be dealt with by the main impi, one at a time. As a strategy of response to the British invasion, it could hardly have been improved upon.

It could be argued that whilst the British invasion plan was romantic at worst or unnecessarily complicated and even fanciful at best, the Zulu defence plan was undeniably pragmatic, sound and logical.

The Zulu King Cetshwayo ordered his main impi to move slowly and his warriors thereby would conserve their strength. He told them that the British soldiers wore redcoats, and these were their enemy. Interestingly the handful of British officers who survived the Isandlwana massacre were wearing blue jackets.

The supreme command of the main army was given to an aged but accomplished chief, **Ntshingwayo kaMahole** who was in his seventies and shared joint command of the main army with **Mavumengwana**, an induna of renown, originally from the isaNgqu regiment and now in his forties and a key figure in the Zulu military. They were to adroitly bring twelve regiments, 20,000 warriors to within striking distance of the British camp at Isandlwana, without his army being discovered. They moved slowly and screened by scouts, passed unnoticed despite Chelmsford's best efforts to discover their whereabouts.

FORMATIONS

The British army around 1879 was beginning to undertake a change in tactics in response to the increasingly accurate modern firepower of the era. Closed rank formations were giving way to a use of open ranks or even skirmish formation. However, it quickly became evident that when fighting the Zulu, the British units needed to adopt infantry versus cavalry formations such as closed ranks and squares and orders were given to this effect throughout the second campaign. Prior to the disaster at Isandlwana though, it had been assumed that British companies of regulars could safely deploy in open or even skirmish order and a few good volleys would see off the natives. Whilst this might have worked against other tribes, it was never going to work against the Zulus.

The classic British bayonet charge was seldom employed during the Zulu war; perhaps because of a wariness of engaging the Zulus in hand-to-hand combat. However, at Holbane, a bayonet charge was used to good effect and one against one, the British were more than a match in hand-to-hand combat against the Zulus. The Martini-Henry rifle came with a very long bayonet and thus it had great reach. The Naval Brigade were even better served as they had sword bayonets that could slash as well as thrust. The greatest danger to the British in hand-to-hand combat rested with having their flanks turned or a single unit being worn down and then over-whelmed by a tidal wave of Zulus.

The British in the first campaign were hampered by a shortage of cavalry and whilst the volunteer irregular cavalry units were first rate at scouting, they could not face down a Zulu charge and their morale quickly collapsed when the going got tough. At Holbane, when push came to shove, the British irregular cavalry routed.

The Zulu had plenty of firearms to hand, but these were generally owned and viewed as status symbols and eschewed by warriors in fighting. The assegai/shield combination had been successful for the Zulu since the Shaka era and there was no attempt by the Zulu to change their strategy in the face of the British threat. That said, a fair few Zulus took rifles into battle and on frequent occasions they would put down enough fire to inflict some British casualties.

The Zulu Impi could move in column or skirmish formation but invariably attacked in closed lines. When on campaign a Zulu army would throw out a field of skirmishers and scouts. The Zulu troops were so disciplined that it was quite possible for large forces to sit silently in long grass, or some concealed location, and the enemy could pass by and not notice them. Once an enemy force had been located the Zulu army would instinctively assume the initiative, either laying an ambush and then awaiting the enemy to walk into a trap or they would launch an attack in the classic formation of the fighting bull buffalo: a centre attack being supported by two flanking attacks and a reserve behind the centre.

The Zulu army morale was very high, even after several defeats they refused to believe that they were not the naturally superior army. In a way therefore, arrogance of superiority affected both the British and Zulu armies alike.

THE WAR

The British invasion plan was based upon a three-pronged advance into Zululand by three columns which would cross the border near the coast in the south, in the centre, at Rorke's Drift, and far inland to the north, in the Transvaal. A fourth, small column would be held in reserve. The plan was devised by the British Commander in Chief, Lord **Chelmsford.** It was perhaps unnecessarily complicated, but Chelmsford's thinking was that by using three columns that gradually converged upon one another, he would trap the Zulu army and thereby force it to do battle. The reality was that with the vast distances between the three columns the Zulus could have, if they had so wished, slipped easily between the columns.

When he took charge of the British forces at the outbreak of the Zulu War Chelmsford was fifty-one. He'd spent more time behind a desk than in the field, but he had seen active service in the Crimea and India. He was regarded as a perfect gentleman and "reliable" was a word often associated with him. He arrived in South Africa in time to conclude one of the last Kaffir wars and was soon after involved in preparations for the Zulu War.

Chelmsford assigned command of the invading columns to Colonels Glyn, Wood and Pearson and gave the reserve column command to Durnford. Some extra British forces were also held in the north at Derby under Colonel Rowlands.

The Central column was commanded by Colonel **Glyn**. Glyn held the command of the 24th Regiment. He was widely regarded as somewhat moody and was frequently at odds with his own officers. Standing just 5'2" tall, he had been bought a commission in the 82nd Regiment by his father as a teenager. He served in the Indian Mutiny, loved hunting and was physically energetic. In 1861 he bought his majority (Major's rank) then in 1867 purchased the rank of Lieutenant Colonel in the 24th Regiment. The Central column would invade Zululand via the drift, or shallow crossing point, on the Buffalo River, alongside a mission station, formerly a farmstead built by an Irishman named Jim Rorke

The Northern column, fifty miles or so further north from Central column, would invade Zululand by crossing the Blood River. The column was commanded by Lieutenant Colonel **Wood**. Born in 1838, Wood held a Victoria Cross. He had a history of ill health and had been injured several times in combat. He had seen active service in numerous campaigns and had already seen service in Africa in the Ashanti War and the last Xhosa campaign.

The Southern (coastal) column was commanded by Colonel **Pearson**. Mentioned in dispatches once, early in his career, Pearson had purchased most of his promotions, as was common, and had briefly retired from the army twice but re-joined to serve in the Zulu War as commander of the coastal column. Pearson would the Tugela River into Zululand close by the coast and his was the closest invasion point from Port Natal (Durban) which lay further to the south.

The reserve column, a weak force indeed was assigned to Colonel **Durnford**. Born in 1830, he came from an army family. He was educated in Germany then went to the Royal Military Academy. He served in Ceylon, developed a penchant for gambling and married young. His wife had an affair. Durnford left her in England while he took postings abroad. In 1865 he had a nervous breakdown. After five years on light duties in England he was posted to Cape Town in 1871. He had never seen active service. In Natal he was involved in leading a force to deal with a rebellious tribe and at Bushman's River Pass his command got into severe difficulties. Durnford himself was speared in the arm. By the time of the Zulu War Durnford had risen to the rank of Lieutenant Colonel but he really had very limited practical military command experience. He had a reputation as a maverick and risk-taker, and he was someone who was keen to prove himself.

There was also a small force under Colonel Rowlands left far up to the north at Luneburg. An isolated spot but not that far from Utrecht, from where Colonel Wood had started out with his northern invasion force.

Chelmsford had what he felt was a marvellously sound plan for the war. He would march upon the Zulu capital and force the Zulu army to battle. His concept of the war was that the Zulus would initially try to hide and adopt hit and run tactics and that the best way to deal with them, was to use numerous columns to "flush them out" and force them to fight. By marching on their capital, he would pressurise them into opposing him. He was doubtless imagining that they would fight a guerrilla war like the Xhosa, whereas in truth the Zulus had no plans to fight like that; they wanted to bring their enemy to battle and destroy them in a decisive confrontation.

Chelmsford believed that once the Zulu army attacked one of his columns it would be shattered by the fire power of the recently introduced breech loading British Martini Henry rifles. These would additionally be supported by artillery and the newly introduced gatling guns. Chelmsford felt he had no worries when it came to fighting the Zulu and his only real concern was in finding enough oxen to pull all the carts and wagons that were needed to shift his army's baggage and equipment.

The Zulu King Cetshwayo nominally commanded around 35,000 troops. When he ordered the army to mobilise, the main Impi assembled at Ulundi and numbered close on 25,000 warriors. Other warriors of affiliated tribes remained scattered across the kingdom. In the far north there were the semi-autonomous AbaQulusi and a small force under an exiled Swazi prince named **Mblini waMswati** who was to prove himself adept in hit and run guerrilla warfare. The main Zulu Impi was placed under a joint command. **Ntshingwayo kaMahole** now in his seventies shared the supreme command with **Mavumengwana**, thirty years his junior and commander of the white shield uThulwana regiment. Whilst

Mavumengwana took shared responsibility for the main army he handed command of the uThulwana regiment, which was his command, to **Dabulamanzi** who was King Cetshwayo's brother. The King's brother was eager to fight the British and was noted for his impetuosity.

January 22nd

Colonel Pearson's southern column was advancing parallel to the coast and making for Eshowe, a disused mission station whose stone buildings had been earmarked to be turned into an advance depot for the column as it moved towards the Zulu capital of Ulundi. Eshowe was roughly thirty-seven miles from the river crossing. At 5am Pearson broke camp and set off on another section of the journey towards Eshowe. Close to the coast the landscape was rush, rolling hills. In the distance, way off to the east, the Indian Ocean could occasionally be glimpsed. The column had been edging forwards since first crossing the border on the 11th. During the crossing of the river Tugela, which denoted the border with Zululand, one sailor had been eaten by a crocodile, but that aside the crossing had been unopposed and since then only small groups of Zulus had been seen in the distance.

The morning of the 22nd was hot with clear skies. By 8am the column had reached a stream, the **Inyezane**, and Pearson called a halt for breakfast. Pearson's force was so large and ponderous that he had split it into two and he had the led the front half forwards and left a gap of distance and time between his half and the second half, reasoning that this would be easier for movement. Ahead lay more hills and forest and it seemed a good spot for the men to stop for breakfast whilst the wagons were brought across the stream.

Pearson had some first-rate troops with him; 400 of his own Regiment, the 3rd, nicknamed "The Buffs", 160 men of the 99th Regiment, 90 Royal Engineers, two 7 pounder guns of the Royal Artillery, a very sizable force of Naval Brigade from HMS Tenedos and HMS Active, who brought with them two 12 pounder guns, two rocket tubes and a gatling gun. In addition, there were over 300 volunteer cavalry and numerous NNC including Natal Native Pioneers to help with the road building tasks. All told he had 4,397 men. 384 ox wagons and 620 civilians served as transportation.

Days earlier, a Zulu Impi, commanded by **Godide kaNdlena** of perhaps 3,000 to 4,000 warriors had branched off from the main Zulu impi after it had left Ulundi and had moved towards the coastal sector to reinforce the local Zulu forces in that area. Godide was Mavumengwana's brother, and he had been given the task of dealing with Pearson's column as best he could with a modest sized forced. He certainly did not have the best regiments of the Zulu war machine, as these had been reserved for the attack against Isandlwana. He commanded the head-ringed inGulube, the iQwa, umXapho, isinGwegwe and the unTsukamngeni. Three of these had been raised after 1856 and thus had seen no active service, as 1856 was the last time that the Zulu war machine had been in action. These three regiments were all made up of men who were now in their forties, so it was inevitable that they would lack the reckless drive of the more youthful regiments. The five regiments Godide had were augmented by local warriors but again these perhaps lacked some discipline, as they were not part of the main Zulu army. It total Godide had perhaps 6,000 to

7,000 warriors and he knew his force had no battle experience. However, Godide, who was around seventy years old had himself seen active service many times including against Boers was determined to do his best and he decided to ambush Pearson whilst he was on the march and when he was crossing the **Inyezane** stream. It was a simple plan but sound plan.

Pearson had broken a simple rule of strategy having split his force in enemy territory before knowing exactly where his enemy were but although he was leading only half of his force, he still had around 2,400 men. Reaching Inyezane at 4.30am he called a halt for breakfast once most of his troops had crossed the stream. He was oblivious of the jaws of the trap that was set around his force but seeing some Zulus scouts in the distance, he sent Lieutenant Hart with one Company of Natal Native Contingent to drive them off. Despite the presence of the Zulu scouts, Pearson was unconcerned and let the men settle down strung out along the track for the breakfast. That the cavalry and mounted infantry had not scouted ahead was negligent in the extreme. Ahead lay an uphill slog and he decided that it would be good for the men to breakfast and rest before making the climb. The land around was mostly thick undergrowth, ravines, spurs of ridges and grassy knolls.

The Zulus scouts fell back as some of the British scouts approached but Hart pushed his NNC on after them. He had around a hundred NNC with him. His natives were clearly agitated and were trying to communicate with the European officers, but these were locally recruited German settlers and there was no common language. The native troops had either sensed the Zulus or spotted them hiding in the thick scrub, but the European officers were oblivious to the fact that they were not just stumbling after a few Zulu scouts, but they were walking into the jaws of an ambush.

Coming out of a ravine, Hart and his men suddenly saw hundreds of Zulus rise up out of the high grass ahead of them. The Natal Native Contingent broke and fled. The handful of European officers and NCOs stood their ground, fired off a few rounds and then were swept aside by the Zulus who left eight British dead behind them as they moved swiftly to attack Pearson's breakfasting troops.

The shots though had alerted Pearson who was quick to deploy the two Companies of Buffs at the front of the column. A hundred Naval Brigade up at the front also quickly fell to and opened fire. Lieutenant Lloyd commanding the artillery at the front though was even quicker to get his guns into action and before the Buffs or Naval Brigade had begun firing, he had unlimbered and fired his opening salvos. The rest of the force was abandoning their breakfast and pulling on their jackets and snatching up their ammunition pouches and Martini-Henry rifles.

Within moments lines of Zulus could be seen curving around the British position and moving against them with disconcerting speed. The sounds of gunfire from the front of the disjointed British force rippled back down the lines. Men who had been bathing in the stream snatched up their belongings as their officers and sergeants barked out orders. The cavalry under Barrow quickly dismounted and opened fire with their carbines and the engineers who had been digging the banks of the stream to make the wagon crossing easier, abandoned their shovels, snatched up rifles and joined in firing at the Zulus who were closing fast on the extended column. Everyone could see what was happening and for the moment the situation seemed to be firmly in the Zulus favour.

The Zulus were moving fast to encircle the British but already they were under heavy fire. The NNC had sprung the trap prematurely. The NNC had discovered the Zulu left horn and in forcing it to charge when it did, the Zulu centre and right horn were minutes behind in co-ordinating their attacks and every minute counted. The Naval Brigade were quick to get the gatling gun brought into action and a moment later two more Companies of The Buffs, rushed into the affray and added more rifle fire into the equation. A moment after that the Naval Brigade rocket launcher scored a lucky hit on a cluster of Zulu warriors.

The Zulu envelopment failed to close and now being met with steady fire and the Zulus realised that the ambush had not worked. The Naval Brigade moved uphill to counterattack supported by The Buffs. There was some sharp fighting and then the Zulus fell back.

Godide had planned an audacious ambush against a strong British force but by 9.30am the British had clearly gained the upper hand and he knew it. He sensibly ordered his warriors to break off the engagement and retire. British casualties numbered just 15 killed. With around 400 dead the Zulus abandoned the fight and fell back to re-group, leaving Pearson able to continue his march to Eshowe.

Pearson had been very lucky though, having been caught out on the march and nearly successfully ambushed. If Godide had had a couple more impis or warriors who were more determined, it is probable that they would have got into hand-to-hand combat and the outcome could have been another Zulu victory. The experience had though certainly unsettled Pearson greatly and reaching **Eshowe**, he quickly set about fortifying the place.

The abandoned mission station stood at 2,000 feet above sea level and comprised a church, a school and a house. There was a grove of orange trees and a stream provided fresh water. Pearson ordered a rectangular fort to be built, which was some 200 yards by 50 yards in size. The six-foot-high walls were loop-holed, and the fort was surrounded by a deep ditch which was filled with spikes. Whilst the British had a formidable force, Pearson adopted to stay forthwith on the defensive and he became pinned down at Eshowe. Godide had a relatively small impi, certainly not enough to attack the well defended camp but he proved more than able to keep Pearson on the back foot and before long the British were suffering casualties from illness as a result of the cramped and unhealthy living conditions. When the British made forays to scout the hills surrounding the mission station they were invariably ambushed by parties of Zulus and soon a feeling of menace hung over the camp which was made worse by the camp being cut off from news from the outside world.

Later the same day, the 22nd, far to the north-west, the British northern column under Colonel Wood crossed the Ncome river and moved against Zulu forces centred upon **Holbane**, a massive flat-topped mountain which commanded the land for miles about.

The first objective Wood set himself was the kraal of Chief Mabamba at Zungwini. Wood sent a strong scouting force forward supported by a few companies of infantry, but the Zulus abandoned the kraal and fell back. Wood pushed on after them.

Wood was keen to get to grips with the Zulus. Leaving just two companies of Regulars at his camp, he now split up his command into three task forces and moved towards Holbane. On reflection, to have divided his force into so many parts in hostile territory and without knowing the enemy strength or true location, was folly. But Wood was, like Chelmsford at this time, scathing about the ability of the Zulu when it came to a fight.

Colonel Buller, commander of Wood's cavalry had 75 men and 7 officers of the Frontier Light Horse and another 22 Boers under their commander Piet Uys moved against Kulabatu, a homestead of a local Zulu chief and after a skirmish which cost the lives of a dozen Zulu and saw just of one the Frontier Light Horse wounded, Buller moved against the summit of a hill a handful of Zulus had retreated to. However, as he advanced, he found hundreds of Zulus moving to encircle his force, so he quickly withdrew. Buller returned to base, one boer had been killed and there were some wounded but he'd got clear of the Zulus who he reckoned numbered close on a thousand.

Wood made another foray against Zungwini hill, this time with a stronger force, where there were around a thousand Zulus, but the Zulus simply melted away. In the distance from the hilltop some of the British cavalry had now reached, they saw, in the distance some 4,000 Zulus parading on top of the Ityanka plateau. They paused and watched whilst the Zulus formed first a circle then a triangle and finally an enormous square. The precision drilling drew complimentary comments from the British officers watching. After some time, the Zulus finished their drilling and headed off towards the massive flat-topped mountain Holbane. It was late in the day, so Wood camped for the night and resumed activities the next day.

The next day as he moved towards Holbane his force came under rifle fire from concealed parties of Zulus and then a force of 4,000 clashed with Companies of the 90th Regiment who deployed in skirmish order put up a strong enough fire to push the Zulus back.

The rest of the afternoon for Wood's forces, was spent in running skirmishes around Holbane with the Zulus. Some 50 Zulus were killed and plenty of cattle captured. Wood was feeling pretty content with the days activities. He had taken forward units of his column deep into Zulu territory and for three days they had been probing further into the Zulu lands, skirmishing with the enemy and capturing cattle. It was, he must have thought, going rather well. Then a lone horsemen, breathless and exhausted rode up with a message. It was now the 24th January and the news was that the camp at Isandlwana had met with disaster.

Wood immediately thought of his own camp back at Khambula, now some three days away and only lightly guarded. He quickly told his officers what had happened and ordered a retreat to khambula. He would make the men march day and night until they were safely back at the camp.

Disaster for the British on January 22nd

Colonel Glyn's central column, accompanied by Lord Chelmsford, moved from Rorke's Drift, where there was a mission station now turned into supply depot and crossed the border river and made its first camp at the base of a large, distinctive mountain called **Isandlwana**. On route the column took time out to attack a kraal belonging to the Induna Sihayo. All the warriors of Sihayo had long ago reported to Ulundi and just old men and boys were left. Some were shot in a one-sided firefight, those that were wounded or surrendered were interrogated. Nothing could be got out of the prisoners however.

The camp site at Isandlwana commanded a good field of view to the east. However, the site was far from perfect, to the north lay the Nquthu plateau, further to the east the Nklandla Hills and to the southeast the Inhlazatshe Hills. The camp was blindsided to the west by the massive mountain Isandlwana itself. The ground was too rocky to dig defensive ditches so, as a precaution, a laager of wagons should have been formed. Chelmsford though decided that it was unnecessary to form a laager, essentially because it was a lot of bother, and he didn't plan on staying in that place for very long.

Reconnaissance in force by the NNC found some Zulus, around 1,500 to the east of Isandlwana and Chelmsford became convinced that this was a screen for the main Zulu army. He split his column, taking half the column in a night march with Colonel Glyn east to reinforce his reconnaissance force of NNC who were there and he left half his force at Isandlwana under the command of Colonel **Pulleine** who was the commander of the first battalion of the 24th. Like Wood to the northwest and Pearson to the south-east, Chelmsford had committed the cardinal sin of splitting his force in enemy territory without having first definitely located his enemy.

Colonel Pulleine was forty years old and had not actually seen any active service. Nevertheless, he was regarded as totally reliable and competent, and Chelmsford was content to leave him in command at the camp. Chelmsford sent an order to Colonel Durnford to move his reserve column up to Isandlwana but neglected to clarify to either Pulleine or Durnford how these two officers of matching rank were to work alongside each other.

On the morning of the 22nd after Chelmsford, with roughly half the column, had long since set off in the dark, the remainder of the camp awoke to what they doubtless imagined was to be another uneventful day.

The feeling was that those left behind at camp were to miss out on the action, in which Chelmsford was in pursuit.

Of the six Companies of Regulars in camp, Lieutenant Pope's 'G' Company was some 1,500 yards north of the camp on outpost duties. These men were strung out in groups of four across a thousand yards. There were also some Natal Native Contingent deployed as outposts to Pope's east and a few mounted vedettes too, who gazed at the empty plateau before them.

At just after 7.30am during breakfast a rider came into camp to report a large body of Zulus on the Nqutu plateau. "Fall in" and "Column Call" were sounded, and 'G' company fell back to join the others in camp. Within ten minutes all six Companies were deployed but with the six other Companies absent, gaps in the lines had to be filled and the men were spread out accordingly.

Shortly after 10.00am Lieutenant Vause was ordered to move his force in response to a Zulu encircling movement which was threatening the camp's rear. Lieutenant Hillier, Captain Essex, Lieutenant Chard and J A Brickhill the interpreter, all also made testimony to Zulus around the camp in the early morning in force. This suggests that forces of Zulu were sighted on the flanks of the camp to the west and east but that the British did not join the dots of their thinking and see that these sightings, many miles apart from each other, were in fact regiments forming the horns of a massive encirclement and that once the horns were in place the chest would show itself on the plateau to the north of camp.

A short while after the Zulus had first been spotted, Durnford rode into camp with his force. Durnford and Pulleine met and discussed the situation but at this point no Zulus could currently be seen from camp. Collectively the British force now numbered close on 900 Europeans and over 1,000 Natal Native Contingent. Durnford was technically in overall command.

Durnford sent two troops of Sikali's Natal Native Horse up onto the plateau to have a scout around. They were commanded by Lieutenants Raw and Roberts. A while later another note came into camp to report Zulus moving from the plateau eastwards.

Durnford elected to ride out of camp in pursuit of these Zulus with his force and at the same time Pulleine decided to send 'A' Company under Cavaye up onto the plateau to support the Natal Native Contingent and vedettes. It was now 11am. Still there was no sign of any Zulus and so the troops in camp were told to "Stand down".

Scouting a seemingly deserted landscape, some four miles from camp, Raw's Mounted Volunteers chanced upon a handful of Zulus herding some cattle. They gave pursuit and the Zulus disappeared over a slope. When Raw's men reined in at the edge of the slope they found themselves looking down into a valley filled with around 15,000 Zulu warriors, sat in complete silence. The valley lay four or five miles from the camp. This was the chest of the Zulu fighting bull buffalo. For a second Raw's men were rooted to the spot and so were the Zulus, but it was only for a second. The Zulu army rose to its feet and moved to the attack. Raw's horsemen turned and retired, firing as they fell back, whilst a few galloped for camp to raise the alarm.

Mehiokazulu KaSihayo, commander of the iNgomakhosi regiment, who was questioned after the war was concluded in November by the Governor of Pietermaritzburg jail and Lieutenant-Colonel Steward stated that he and three other chiefs were sent to scout the British camp very early in the morning of the 22nd and when they made their report to Ntshingwayo, he made the decision then to move against the British camp. So, what appears likely is that Ntshingwayo ordered the regiments assigned to the horns to move into place during the early hours of the morning as they had the furthest distance to cover and that the chest regiments were made to wait while the horns moved into position. Raw had stumbled upon the chest and in so doing he precipitated the advance of the chest.

For Chelmsford to have split his force in enemy territory, before he knew for certain where the enemy were and in what strength, was irresponsible in the extreme. His intelligence was faulty, and he had incorrectly joined the dots together. The Zulus had, by chance, wrong footed the British. The main Zulu army was not away to the east, it was in fact encamped just to the north of Isandlwana.

Pulleine and Durnford had also failed to join the dots. When Zulus in force had first been sighted to the flanks of the British camp, that was the time that the British should have acted. Rather than assume they could defend the perimeter of the camp with half of the force having left the camp (with Chelmsford), Pulleine should have reduced his perimeter accordingly. Likewise, Durnford should not have wilfully scattered his command by embarking on some wild goose chase. He should have remained in camp and prepared a defensive position.

So, on the same day that Colonel Pearson had his battle at Inyezane and Colonel Wood had his battle to the north around Holbane, Pulleine and Durnford were going to have a battle on their hands too.

Durnford's decision to, rather than remaining in camp, ride east in pursuit of some elusive Zulu force of unknown size was a reprehensible decision. His force rapidly became strung out across the plain, the rocket launcher unit becoming quite detached from his cavalry. Durnford's actions were quite irresponsible because he was disregarding his orders to stay in camp to support Pulleine and he was also being naïve in the extreme, if he imagined he had any chance of successfully engaging a large Zulu force with his limited resources.

It is quite extraordinary to think that Durnford was willing to disregard his orders to reinforce the camp and that Pulleine was willing to let him do this.

At around midday twelve Zulu regiments, fully 20,000 warriors, perhaps more, poured towards the British camp. Pulleine could see that away to the north 'A' Company was industriously firing at some target, but the target could not be seen from down at camp. Pulleine now made his next mistake, deciding to send a second Company, 'F'

Company under Captain Mostyn up onto the escarpment to join 'A' Company.

When Mostyn reached 'A' company and saw what they were up against he ordered both Companies to begin to retire upon the camp, firing as they withdrew. Meanwhile back in camp Pulleine saw the two Companies to the north retreating in the direction of the camp. He then made his next mistake, he sent a third Company, 'C' Company out of camp to go and support them. At the base of the plateau the three Companies formed up facing north and the remaining three Companies in camp then formed up facing the east, so that the six British Companies of regulars presented an "L" with its sides facing north and east and with the mountain of Isandlwana to the west of the deployment.

The six British Regular Companies under Pulleine were stretched far too thinly. Basically, the six hundred men were spread across a mile. This original line of defence might have been acceptable before Chelmsford had stripped six other Companies from the camp. Now though, it was untenable. "H" Company under Wardell was probably the most thinly deployed with six yards between each man. The British deployment was exacerbated by the fact that the rear of the British camp lay unprotected and that the west side of the camp was blindsided by the mountain of Isandlwana. Far out across the plain was Durnford's disjointed command.

Much blame has been laid on the British defeat because of a shortage of ammunition and of quartermasters struggling to unscrew the six screws that sealed down each ammunition box and to then remove the two copper bands which further secured the box. This does not stand up to scrutiny. Each ammunition box, in point of fact, had a sliding central compartment that was held in place with just one screw. There wasn't even a need to unscrew it; a heavy bash with the end of a Martini-Henry or a rock would bend the screw and free the compartment. Recent surveying of the battlefield shows numerous bent screws and pull handles from the foil inner compartment of the ammunition boxes distributed around the British firing line, so it seems certain that there was not an ammunition shortage at the front line.

The new Martini-Henry rifle was also blamed for the British defeat with claims that it over-heated and cartridges jammed. This was not a problem however at any other battle, although the guns did get hot and cartridges could jam, this is about as convincing as the Zulus blaming a defeat on a windy day spoiling their spear throwing.

The Natal Native Contingent also have come in for some of the blame. Some Companies of NNC were allegedly left deployed, slightly forward of the British regular Companies at the knuckle between the two lines facing north and east. Some writers suggest that when these NNC troops broke, they created a gap in the British line through which the Zulus poured. This claim does not stand up to detailed scrutiny.

The British defeat at Isandlwana must rest firmly with the two Colonels present. Colonel Pulleine for deploying his troops piecemeal and without even personally fully evaluating the enemy threat. Colonel Durnford for disregarding orders by leaving the camp.

Durnford would also make matters worse by later withdrawing from his position without giving any notice of intentions to the British regulars supporting his flank. Whilst his men had horses and were able to ride back towards camp, the British infantry Company covering his flank was suddenly left exposed to envelopment.

Perhaps and most crucially was the truth that the British senior commanders, Pulleine and Durnford, didn't have the imagination to see that they were staring disaster in the face. The letters of Henry Curling of the Royal Artillery and one of the very few to survive the massacre that ensued gives a good insight into what went wrong. Quite simply put the officers all believed that the Zulus would behave like all the other native forces that they had encountered in Africa. The British officers were quite convinced that their enemy would charge pell-mell only to be scattered by a few volleys of controlled rifle fire. In the first major engagement of the war the British simply under-estimated their adversary and they paid the price.

Ntshingwayo had made his plan of attack and every regimental commander knew what he had to do. The Zulu regiments swung into action seamlessly. In stark contrast the British were improvising minute by minute and the two Colonels were not even reading from the same battle plan. The Zulu army streamed south, the regiments that comprised the centre heading straight for the British camp. The regiments that formed the left horn were swinging well south and in so doing they came into contact with Durnford's troops. The Zulu right horn had swung far around behind the Isandlwana mountain to complete the encirclement. While the British might just have had enough troops to hold a line to the north and east they had left their west and south completely unguarded. The British deployment was a disaster waiting to happen.

In the centre of the Zulu attack were the Uve regiment, the umHlanga regiment, the umCijo regiment and the white shield isAnagqu regiment. These were the regiments that spear-headed the attack. However, they only carefully skirmished forwards whilst giving time for the other regiments to complete the encirclement. It is worth quoting at this point Henry Curling for he wrote: "All the time we were idle in camp, the Zulus were surrounding us with a huge circle several miles in circumference and hidden by hills from our sight. None of us felt the least anxious as to the result for, although they came on in immense numbers, we felt it was impossible they could force a way through us."

Curling's words raise an interesting question: for how long were the British "idle" in camp? The truth was that the Zulus had indeed been encircling the camp since early in the morning, but the British were none to bothered by this or as Curling puts it; "none of us felt the least anxious".

Captain Edward Essex of the 75th who was Colonel Glyn's transport officer wrote that the Zulus moved in to around a 1,000 yards distance from the British firing line and then "they did not advance but moved steadily towards our left, each man running from rock to rock...with the evident intention of outflanking us... they skirmished beautifully, and I saw that very few, considering we now had about 3000 opposed to us, were hit."

The Zulu main attack did not come until the entire Zulu army was fully deployed and had completely encircled the British camp. By this time the Zulus regiments facing the British firing line had edged forward until 500 yards or less separated them from the British firing line. Whilst the British kept up a steady but probably ineffectual fire against the skirmishing Zulus, the distance was closed even further. Mostly, the Zulus were lying down now and crawling forwards and the British fire was achieving little. It was around 2pm.

Pulleine had around 1,800 troops at his disposal, but he had spread them too thinly and disaster was looming. Perhaps he thought though he was giving the Zulus a jolly good pasting and that natives lying on the bellies in the grass were never going to really threaten the camp. He probably also never believed that a native force could be disciplined enough and have sufficient grasp of strategy and tactics to effectively manage an encirclement across several miles by a dozen regiments who totalled well over 20,000 men. Nevertheless, this is what the Zulus did.

It was mid-afternoon and the British Regular companies along with the mounted volunteers had deployed themselves into a long line facing north and then facing east and were firing steadily at the Zulu regiments facing them. The Zulus were using the cover, scrub, dongas and such like as best they could to avoid the relentless fire from the British and most of the Zulus were probably lying down, crouching and edging forwards as best they could. Gradually the Zulus edged south and pushed closer, using the broken ground to their advantage. Pulleine, seeing how thinly his front-line troops were spread ordered every man still in camp capable of bearer arms to move out and join the firing line.

The umCijo regiment and the uMbonambi were first to charge into hand-to-hand combat against the British. J F Brickhill an interpreter, who was one of the few lucky survivors, wrote: "At 150 yards they raised a shout of 'usutu'. They then came on with an overwhelming rush." The umCijo were a black shield regiment raised in 1867 and they numbered around 2,500 warriors, most between twenty-eight and thirty years of age. They charged Cavaye's 'A' Company. The speed of the attack was shocking, and the weight of the onslaught was too much for Cavaye's men, who were swiftly overwhelmed. The assured pasting of the native adversaries by the disciplined British force with all their modern firepower suddenly evaporated.

Following the lead set by the umCijo, the rest of the Zulu regiments charged. The British defensive line was smashed to pieces. Pockets of British Regulars fought back-to-back in hastily formed platoon strong squares. Those that could tried to fall back. Handfuls of camp followers stood and fought in defensive circles, but organised and cohesive defence was gone.

While the remnants of the six companies of British Regulars fought on as a handful of dislocated groups, a stream of men, mostly camp followers, wagon drivers, native levies but some Regular troops as well fled south. Amongst them the artillery which saw disaster looming and wanted to save their guns. It could be argued that it was a rout even though some junior officers held together bands of men who stood and fought to last.

The camp had been held by 1,800 men but by late afternoon just fifty-five Europeans, who managed to escape, remained alive. Durnford and Pulleine were both dead. The two artillery pieces in the camp had been captured along with a thousand breech loading Martini Henry rifles and the column's entire ammunition reserve. As a disaster, for the British Victorian army, against a native foe, it was almost without parallel, and it threw the British invasion plan of Zululand into complete disarray.

It is worth considering that if the Zulu main impi had not attacked Isandlwana but had instead engaged Chelmsford, who had a similar number of troops, in all probability, Chelmsford's command would have met a similar fate. Chelmsford, at this time was naïve enough to imagine that he could surprise the enemy and outmanoeuvre them. He also evidently considered that six companies of regulars were enough to take on the Zulu army. He had taken six with him and had left six in camp. He clearly believed 6 Companies was enough to do battle against the Zulus but he was very much mistaken. Given that British assets at Isandlwana actually totalled 1,800 men, it is evident that Chelmsford had totally under-estimated the Zulu danger.

The disaster at Isandlwana dispelled any notion amongst the British senior officers that they could engage the enemy with their own troops simply in skirmish order or open line or fight a fluid battle. In future, secured flanks and rear were imperative. Therefore, a British square was, henceforth, regarded as the best option.

But as bad as Islandwana was for the British the day was not yet finished. Fugitives fled back down the track to Rorke's Drift but only to find it blocked by the waiting inDluwengwe Regiment purposely deployed to head off any such retreat. Raised in 1866, this black shield Regiment were men in their late twenties, they numbered several thousand and were keen to wash their spears. Very few of the British made it past their spears. A second escape route via what became known as Fugitive's Drift was to be the one chance for escape but as the men ran this way the Zulus pursued them. A few British made it to the river and made it across. They stumbled on to Rorke's Drift and to Helpmakaar and the news they brought was to spread like wildfire down the dirt road and back to Durban and rest of the colony.

The Zulu reserve not involved in the fight at Isandlwana went on to **Rorke's Drift** to "wash their spears". There were four regiments; the middle-aged married men of the white shield uThulwana, numbering 1,500, the iNdlondlo raised in 1857 with their distinctive red and white shields who became a regiment of married men in 1876, the Udloko raised in 1858 and numbering 2,000 warriors and they were joined by the iNdluyengwe who had little to do thus far except cut down fugitives trying to escape the slaughter of Isandlwana.

The Zulus were commanded by Prince Dabulamanzi kaMpande, the king's younger brother. This was not by design but by chance. The command had been held of the Reserve by Zibhebhu but he had been wounded and so handed command over to the king's younger brother. Prince Dabulamazi was spoiling for a fight and didn't want the men under his command to miss out on a chance to gain glory.

The depot at Rorke's Drift was under the command of Major Spalding. It was garrisoned by just one Company of Regulars, B Company numbering 94 men, under thirty-five-year-old Lieutenant Bromhead. The Company should have been commanded by the more senior officer Company commander Godwin-Austin but he'd been accidentally wounded by a shot from a rifle by one of his own men. Bromhead was a good enough chap, but he was a tad deaf, so a quiet posting behind the action seemed eminently suitable for him in the eyes of Chelmsford. There was also a Lieutenant Chard of the Engineers there, working on building a river crossing. He had with him five sappers and two natives. Chard had seen no combat action. The mission station was little more than two thatched roof stone houses that lay in the western lee of a commanding hill. The Zulus called it Shiyane. The one-time resident a Swedish missionary, Otto Witt, had named it the Oscaberg, in honour of his king. The British had established a supply depot and a makeshift hospital at Rorke's Drift. There were around thirty patients. They were looked after by thirty-five-year-old Surgeon James

Henry Reynolds. Reynolds had seen his share of active since. There were also a few hundred NNC present at the base. All told Major Spalding had around 400 men.

On the morning of the 22nd Chard had ridden from Rorke's Drift up the camp at Isandlwana on business and was back at Rorke's Drift around midday and at around that time the sound of distant firing could be heard at Rorke's Drift coming from the direction of Isandlwana. Major Spalding, anxious about a re-supply issue, left Rorke's Drift at 2pm to ride back to the tiny outpost at Helpmakaar twelve miles down the road to see if he could chase up the delayed convoy of wagons and men that were due. Not long after he had left, two Lieutenants of the NNC, Vane and Ardendorf rode into Rorke's Drift. They brought the unbelievable news that the camp at Isandlwana had been utterly overrun by a vast Zulu horde.

Chard, Bromhead and Reynolds held a rapid council of war. Acting Assistant Commissary Dalton was also present. Dalton was now serving as a volunteer, but he had a Regular army career stretching starting back 1849 through the 1871 when he retired with the rank of staff sergeant. Bromhead knew and respected him, and Dalton was a shrewd and calm man who commanded the officers' respect. The decision was made not to evacuate the camp and risk being caught in the open but to stand and fight. There were substantial supplies of mealie bags and biscuit boxes at the base, and these were used to hastily fortify the base by building walls with them to connect the two buildings and form a defensive space. The officers knew the Zulus could arrive at any time.

How many Zulus, they had no idea, perhaps the entire force that had slaughtered their comrades at Isandlwana a few hours earlier? 1,400 men had been lost just a few miles away and it looked like they were next and the numbered just 400 and were without artillery and cavalry. The sense of urgency bordering on panic to build some defences must have been unbearable.

The two main buildings stood thirty-five yards apart with the hospital lying to the north-west of the storehouse. Adjacent to the storehouse was a cattle kraal, well built. Further to the north-east there was another stock pen, less well built. To the north of the hospital and storehouse there was a five-foot-high stone wall, some scrub beyond it and then the dirt road and beyond that a ditch and then an orchard. To the south of the two building the ground rose up to Shiyane or the Oskaberg hill. As a defensive position it was somewhere between bad and terrible.

The decision was made to throw-up a mealie bag wall up just the north of the two buildings and construct another wall to connect buildings on the south side. Whilst these hastily improvised walls were being made, Colour Sergeant Bourne was sent out with a couple of men to keep a look out for the Zulus. During the early afternoon stragglers from the chaos of Isandlwana staggered into Rorke's Drift in ones and twos. All brought stories of the disaster and most then quickly slipped away on to Helpmakaar the pretext of going to warn the small garrison there. A force of native horse came in under Lieutenant Vause but their nerves were in shreds and after a short interval they rode off. The NNC at the base sensing the hopeless of the situation ran off as well. It was a bitter blow for Chard and Bromhead. Their meagre force of around 400 was suddenly now just 140 and of these there were only 81 fighting fit men of B Company to form a dependable core. Then just to add to their sense of woe before the walls had been completed a cry rang out from one of the men sent to look out for the approaching enemy announcing that the Zulus were coming.

Whilst the situation for the British looked dire they did have a few things going in their favour. Firstly, the Zulus were led by an impetuous hot-head who was too impatient to stop and think-out a proper plan of battle. Second, the British had a vast store of ammunition. Thirdly, they did have a defensive perimeter and as the battle developed, some men were assigned to improving it.

The ensuring battle raged from mid-afternoon until the early hours of the next day. From behind their makeshift defences the British held off a series of determined but piecemeal Zulu attacks. The Zulus gradually wore the defenders down although their casualties were appalling. First the hospital was abandoned and another defensive line thrown up closer to the storehouse. Then, holding this reduced perimeter became too stressful and Chard had a final mealie bag redoubt thrown up in-front of the storehouse. Here the British would make their last stand.

The quantities of ammunition expended was enormous. The single Company of men had drawn on an entire Battalion's reserve some thirty-four boxes of cartridges but now only six boxes remained. They had fired 25,000 rounds. The rifles were glowing hot and the barrels were thick with carbon. And if they kept on like this, they would run out ammunition in two more hours firing. The water was gone, the men had been fighting continuously for close on twelve hours. Chard and Bromhead had lost 17 men and many more were wounded. The British were close to breaking-point, but they had to fight on, because there was no other choice. But the Zulus too were exhausted. Three or four hundred warriors lay dead or dying. The Zulus decided to withdraw in the early hours of the morning and Chard, Bromhead and the exhausted survivors at Rorke's Drift were left to tend to their wounded and to await a relief force. It had been, on the face of it, a miraculous story of survival

However, on reflection is fair to say that it was good British leadership and poor Zulu leadership at Rorke's Drift gave the chance for a hundred plus British soldiers to inflict heavy casualties on a Zulu force of 4,000 warriors. Bromhead and Chard sensibly kept their scant force behind an encircling defensive makeshift wall and standing shoulder to shoulder the Company of Regulars poured a continuous fire into the Zulus who had made a series of determined but poorly co-ordinated charges against the mission station.

If the Zulus had not been commanded by the impetuous Dabulamanzi but had been led by a shrewder commander such as Prince Mblini waMswati the outcome may have been very different. As it was, the survival of the defenders, against seemingly overwhelming odds, was a crumb of comfort for the emotionally shattered Lord Chelmsford. It is also worth noting that whilst British infantry marched with 70 rounds of ammunition, during the fight at Rorke's Drift, 140 men used 20,000 rounds of ammunition in a firefight that raged for roughly twelve hours. It was fortunate for Chard's little force that they were sitting on a decent chunk of a full battalion's reserve of ammunition. Each man on average had fired close on 150 rounds, more than double the normal allocation.

After the four battles of the 22nd of January the war went into a period of inactivity. The Zulu main army retired first to the Royal capital and then dispersed to rest and recover. Zulu casualties ran to over 2,000 and Cetshwayo was deeply upset by this. He felt that an assagai had been thrust into the belly of the Zulu people. Nevertheless, his army had blunted the British invasion of his country.

Chelmsford was in a state of shock following the disaster at Isandlwana. He withdrew what was left of central column back into Natal and he requested more troops from London and then set about evaluating what he could do next. He was so humiliated by the loss of most of central column that when he wrote to Pearson, he could at first only bring himself to report the loss of Durnford's troops and the full disaster of Isandlwana was not explained to Pearson until later. When he wrote again to Pearson, he told him to either stay put at Eshowe or to abandon it. He told Pearson that he could do whatever he thought best but he was warned to expect the full force of the Zulu war machine to come down on him. It was, if you read Chelmsford's letters at this time to Pearson as if Chelmsford was at a lost. His confidence was shattered.

Pearson was now too anxious to move out from Eshowe. Doubtless he imagined the full force of the Zulu war machine descending upon him. In truth however, Pearson was to be harassed by now more than a modest Zulu force, but he assumed the worst. It is as if he was infected by Chelmsford's sense of anxiety and melancholy. He dug in and prepared for siege with a reduced garrison. Retaining 1,300 troops in the fort he ordered the return of his cavalry and Natal Native Contingent to Natal. In truth it was a retreat. Reluctant or too afraid to pick up the baton that Chelmsford had dropped, he passed the initiative the Zulus.

It is interesting to conjecture about what might have happened if Pearson had decided to make a solo push for Ulundi. He was after all a third of the way there having reached as far as Eshowe. He had a large force; 1,600 Natal Native Contingent, 312 cavalry, artillery, rocket launchers, a gatling gun, Naval Brigade and Regulars. In total 4,400 men. He had repulsed the Zulu's once. The main Zulu impi after Isandlwana had dispersed and had suffered heavy casualties. It must obviously remain an unanswerable "what-if?" but might be something perhaps for the wargamer to re-enact. I believe that if Pearson had pushed for Ulundi, he probably would have got there and possibly shortened the Zulu war by four or more months. However, he opted for extreme caution, and he chose to divide his force, so that he had less mouths to feed at Eshowe. He sent his cavalry and NNC back to Natal and he dug-in and awaited events to unfold. He allowed his force at Eshowe to become cut-off, handing the initiative to the Zulus.

It seems to me that Pearson was panicked into a decision by Chelmsford's doom and gloom warning that he was "on his own". He could have opted to pull back his entire force to Natal, which might have been a sensible precaution because he could then at least attempt to protect Natal from a Zulu incursion. Or he could, having fortified Eshowe, left it garrisoned and continued his advance towards Ulundi, thereby pressurising the Zulus and hopefully taking some pressure off the other British units left defending the border.

It is interesting to note also that Pearson did not make a command decision on what course to take but he discussed it with all his officers, seeking their advice. This strikes one as a man racked with indecision and uncertainty. From Eshowe there was a track leading to a mission station called St Pauls. Between the two places there were two rivers to cross. After St Paul's there was just 25 miles and two more rivers to cross before Ulundi. Not easy going for a convoy of heavy wagons but certainly not impossible. In the event, when Chelmsford was to launch his second invasion on Zululand, he would choose a route that was nearly three times as long as this and far worse. This decision was made because Chelmsford refused to march on the most direct route to the Zulu capital, as this meant facing the ghosts at Isandlwana.

For Pearson, soon the hills around the mission station at Eshowe were dotted with Zulus. British runners sent with messages back to Natal failed to make the journey. Patrols came under attack from groups of Zulus. It became evident that Eshowe was effectively isolated and in a state of siege. Before the siege was to be lifted, twenty-six troops were to die from sickness and most of the remainder were in ill-health. Pearson's decision to stay put at Eshowe served no beneficial purpose, it did not tie down the Zulu main army which meantime moved west against Wood. Pearson's assets trapped at Eshowe now became a liability that needed to be rescued.

To summarise the situation after the opening moves in the war: Chelmsford had split his force in the middle and half of it was destroyed along with all the supplies for the whole column. Wood's northern force had so far accomplished little. Pearson's coastal column was split. Half was trapped at Eshowe, the rest had retreated to British territory. It was not an auspicious start for the British. It seemed that with Chelmsford's central column in disarray and Pearson hemmed in at Eshowe, the only person who could do anything constructive was Wood. No surprise therefore that received letters from Chelmsford telling him to "do something." Exactly what was left to Wood to decide but it as made clear that he was expected to do something and suddenly the spotlight was thrown upon Wood. For the moment it seemed to the British that the Zulu army was in the ascendancy.

However, the Zulu situation was far from perfect. They had taken heavy casualties at three battles, Isandlwana, Rorke's Drift and Inyezane. Yes, the had blunted the British invasion, indeed they had temporarily halted it. However, the Zulu army needed to recoup and rest and Cetshawayo was loath to take the war across the river and into Natal. He decided that he would let his main impi rest for a time and then launch it again at the British.

Given that the British near the coast were showing no signs of advancing and had indeed pulled back many of their soldiers, there was only one logical course of action. He would send his army north-west against Wood.

But whilst the British were gathering reinforcements and the main Zulu impi was recovering from the trauma of the 22nd, other Zulus units were not inactive. In March, Prince Mblini waMswati led a small force of his pro-Zulu warriors on a lightning raid across the border. At **Ntombe** he ambushed a company of the 80th Regiment in a night-time raid deep into British territory and scored a small but notable Zulu victory, wiping out almost a full company of British regulars. It seems likely that a single native who, it was noted, had joined the British camp for supper and sat amongst the British native levies was Mblini himself, come to spy out the enemy before slipping away and then directing his night-time attack.

By the end of March, encouraged by Chelmsford and in attempt to wrest back the initiative from the Zulus, Colonel Wood mounted an attack against the Zulus in the north. Wood decided to use all his cavalry and some native forces in a lightning raid against the mountain fastness of **Holbane.** Wood felt that this was an easily managed operation that would deal a blow to the Zulus. There was a large force on Holbane but nothing that he couldn't deal with.
Chelmsford had written to Wood saying that he believed the main Zulu army, if it had re-assembled, was actually moving far to the south against Pearson at Eshowe and so Wood should have no more Zulus to bother with than the northern forces he had already once skirmished with.

Wood, sanctioned and encouraged by Chelmsford made his plans. Wood though was to make mistakes that were to cost him dearly. He chose not to undertake a reconnaissance of Holbane and formulated an elaborate plan: a night-time march with a split force and a surprise attack on the Zulus at Holbane. Holbane was a vast mountain plateau and he believed that there were two paths leading to the summit one at one end and one at the other.

He assembled 600 troops, including nearly all his cavalry, for the raid. His force would move on the mountain at night, split in two and ascend the mountain by the two paths in the early hours of the morning, catching the Zulus by complete surprise. The Zulus would be trapped on the top and he would destroy them.

At the eleventh hour of preparations, he received a report that the main Zulu army had indeed reassembled and was in fact making north against his force rather than south to attack Pearson. Wood foolishly still decided though that he had enough time to continue with his plan and be back at his base long before the Zulu main army would be in his vicinity. How he made this assessment, we don't know but he was wrong.

After a night-time march, the two British forces were in place at either end of Holbane, only to find that at one end there was actually no feasible rout up to the summit. Nevertheless, the troops at the northern end of Holbane began to fight their way uphill against small groups of Zulus hidden in caves and behind defensive rock and stone walls that guarded the snaking path that climbed to the mountain's summit. The Zulus who were on Holbane were under the joint command of Sikhobobo and Prince Mblini waMswati who directed his men to melt away into the undergrowth and caves rather than try to fight the British head on once they had reached the summit.

By the time the British had ascended Holbane from the north they had taken casualties but felt pleased with themselves. However, the vast plateau appeared deserted. Gingerly they moved from the north end of the plateau, which actually extended for miles, southwards, searching in vain for the Zulu force they had come to beat-up. The sides of the plateau dropped as sheer rock faces to the west and east. Utterly impassable terrain, they noted. The only way was south or to go back north. There was no sign of anything more than a handful of Zulus and a few herds of cattle. They pressed on southwards but then one of the riders, glancing back over his shoulder saw to his horror a vast impi away to the north-east and moving with startling speed to Holbane. It was the main Zulu impi.

Wood had disregarded his intelligence that the main Zulu impi was indeed closing on him and he naively assumed he had time to conduct his surprise raid on Holbane. However, he was now caught with half his force trapped on the top of the mountain and the rest of his force split between his camp and scattered around Holbane.

The British horsemen were hopelessly outnumbered and isolated on the summit of Holbane, whose sheer cliff faces made escape, except by the narrow path they had ascended, impossible. However, it looked certain that the

Zulu army would reach the northern base of Holbane before they could retrace their steps, so most opted to gallop the length of Holbane, some four miles and exit by the southern path where of course they imagined the rest of the British would have ascended by. The southern path however turned out to be no more than a series of sheer rock steps and was hopelessly perilous. If the British had scouted this out beforehand, they would have seen this but Wood had neglected to do this. It had looked like a path from a far through binoculars and that had been good enough. Now the British on the top of Holbane was trapped and were in a state of panic. Seeing help was at hand with the arrival of the main Zulu impi, Mblini's Zulus poured out of their hiding places and began to mercilessly pursue the retreating, disordered British as they first swung north then saw that there was never enough time to retrace their steps in that direction and then swung swung south and fled pell-mell down a mountain path that was little more than a death trap for panicked, rushing horsemen. The British retreat disintegrated into a rout. Fifteen officers and over a hundred horsemen were killed. The Natal Native Contingent units involved in the raid lost two thirds of their men. The Zulu impi enveloped the mountain and they hounded the British as they fled back towards their camp. Wood's plan was in tatters. Wood himself was so shaken by the turn of events that for a time he wandered unable to take control of the deteriorating situation and even unable to return immediately to his camp at Kambula to organise preparations to face the inevitable Zulu onslaught. Late in the day he returned to Kambula and digging deep into his mental reserves he pulled himself together and prepared for the battle that was to come.

Kambula – the turning point in the war.

The next day, March 29th, the Zulu main army launched a full attack against the remainder of Wood's column which was camped at **Kambula.** Wood had chosen a good defensive hilltop position and very sensibly this time he kept his force of 2,000 men in a compact defensive position. On the 29th Colonel Wood had definitely got his act together and he was ready to face what was to happen. He had sent cavalry scouts out in the morning and evaluated where the Zulus were and what their strength was. He then brought all his men back into the defensive perimeter including some who had been out gathering firewood. He then ordered the men to have their lunch, knowing that there was time for this, and such actions would send a clear signal to his men that Wood was in control of events. In the early afternoon the Zulus, in five columns, came into sight and closed on Kambula. Wood was ready for them.

For four hours the Zulus tried and failed to smash Wood's force. Formed into a defensive square behind a redoubt and backed by artillery the British held back repeated Zulus charges by disciplined volley fire. When the Zulus did gain the summit from the south, a bayonet charge by two companies of the 90th drove them back. When the Zulus broke off the engagement, they had lost some 2,000 men and yet Wood's casualties were just 28 killed and 55 wounded. When the Zulus began to retreat, Wood ordered the cavalry out to harass them and much of the Zulu retreat was turned into a rout. At long last the British had scored a notable victory and the Zulu main impi had tasted its first defeat.

The Second Invasion

By April Chelmsford had received reinforcements and had reorganised his forces sufficiently to send a fresh column into Zululand to relieve Pearson's force at Eshowe.

A Zulu army under the Induna **Somopo** numbering 10,000 warriors was assembled to confront Chelmsford. The British relief column formed up into one large square once they knew the Zulus were at hand. **Gingindlovu** was another decisive British victory, the Zulus, faced by closed ranks of regulars firing volleys, failed to get into hand-to-hand combat and they abandoned the fight after just twenty minutes, leaving close on 1,000 dead behind. Chemlsford marched on to Eshowe and ordered Pearson to abandon the camp. The fortifications were pulled down and the entire force pulled back to Natal. This is curious and probably reflected Chelmsford fear that the Zulus were still capable of inflicting a major defeat on his forces.

Back in Natal Chelmsford was content to wait as yet more and more British troops and reinforcements poured into the colony. In May he invaded Zululand for a second time. Chelmsford took command of one column, named the 2nd Division and a second column, titled the 1st Division, was led by Colonel Crealock. Wood's column remaining at Kambula was renamed the Flying Column and was brought into a co-ordinated advance with Chelmsford column. The combined 2nd Division and Flying Column advanced upon the Zulu capital, Ulundi, where the final major battle of the war took place

Ulundi. The British numbering around 5,000 men formed in a vast square, bolstered by a dozen field guns and two machine-gatling guns, saw off a Zulu force of around 20,000 warriors who, for thirty minutes, tried and failed to get into hand-to-hand combat. Once the Zulu attack collapsed and the Zulus retreated, Chemlsford opened his square to allow his cavalry out. A charge by the 17th Lancers turned the Zulu retreat into a rout. The Natal Native Contingent was then allowed to pursue the broken Zulu forces and to kill any Zulu wounded that they could find.

Chelmsford was shortly after replaced by General Wolseley as commander in chief who was left to conclude the war and to capture Cetshwayo. Much criticism was levelled at Chelmsford for his conduct of the war, but he survived this, thanks to having Queen Victoria as a friend and having managed at last, at Ulundi, to achieve what could be seen as the final victory over the Zulu nation.

The Zulu King Cetshwayo had warned his army not to attack the British when they were in a defended position. His army disregarded his advice at Kambula and Gingindlovu and paid the price. After two such defeats in pitched battle, it was evident to both sides that the war had clearly turned in the British favour. At Ulundi the

Zulus had tried for a final time to smash a British force is a defensive formation and they failed. Cetshwayo feld northwards and his army scattered. The war was essentially over.

It is interesting to speculate how the war might have progressed had the Zulu contented themselves with more hit and run affairs such as Ntombe and had only made massed attacks on the British columns when they were strung out on a line of march. If the British Colonels and their General had had their faults, so too did some of the Zulu commanders who seemed to prefer the noble glory of a head on pitched battle, to the more realistically viable alternative of "hit and run" tactics.

From a wargaming perspective, in writing the rules that follow, I have tried to create a fair and realistic opportunity for either a Zulu or British victory. The big challenge for wargaming this era is in having a wargaming table that is big enough to allow for the ambitious encircling tactics that the Zulus used. If you keep in mind that their army at Isandlwana was spread out across a front that stretched for five miles, you can see the challenge to the wargamer! So, to try to help with this, the rules have two sets of move/fire ranges. One in inches for larger table-tops and one in centimetres for more modest size wargame tables.

Of course, fighting a small set piece engagement such as Ntombe, where there are perhaps five hundred Zulus attacking one Company of British regulars, table size is not problematic. The challenge comes when one wants to fight a battle more like Isandlwana.

I have tried and tested the rules many times now and each time, I find some instance where a rule modification seems a good idea. You will doubtless find this too. I have tried also to make the rules not too time consuming. Using these rules, you can fight a battle with both sides fielding well over a thousand points and expect to finish the battle quite comfortably within a day. With a 7'6" by 6' table I found there was space enough for a Zulu impi of six, seven or eight thousand warriors, represented by 600 – 800 figures, to engage a British force of matching size and for the Zulus to have just space enough to manoeuvre.

~~~

THE WARGAME RULES

SCALES

1 British figure = 8 men
1 Zulu figure = 10 men
1 artillery piece = 2 artillery guns

This game is designed principally for use with 20mm, 25mm or 28mm figures. The two sets of rules for movement and firing ranges give you the option to choose your preference based on what size figures you have, how long you want the wargame to last and what size wargame table you have.

Base sizes are something that as a wargamer I have been flexible on, as long as forces look right, then as long as opposing forces are based on similar lines, I am content. The challenge with basing Zulus is that they fought both in skirmish order and closed order but moving large impis that are based for skirmish order can take forever. I wargame with 25mm MiniFigs so I have opted to base most of an impi in 4 figures on a single base with a 25mm frontage per figure and depth of 30mm per figure and two rows deep plus a minority of the impi as individual or in twos. British bases are 25mm frontage by 40mm, cavalry 25mm frontage by 65mm and artillery 80mm by 60mm. I have used round based for senior officers and Zulu regimental commanders for ease of identification.

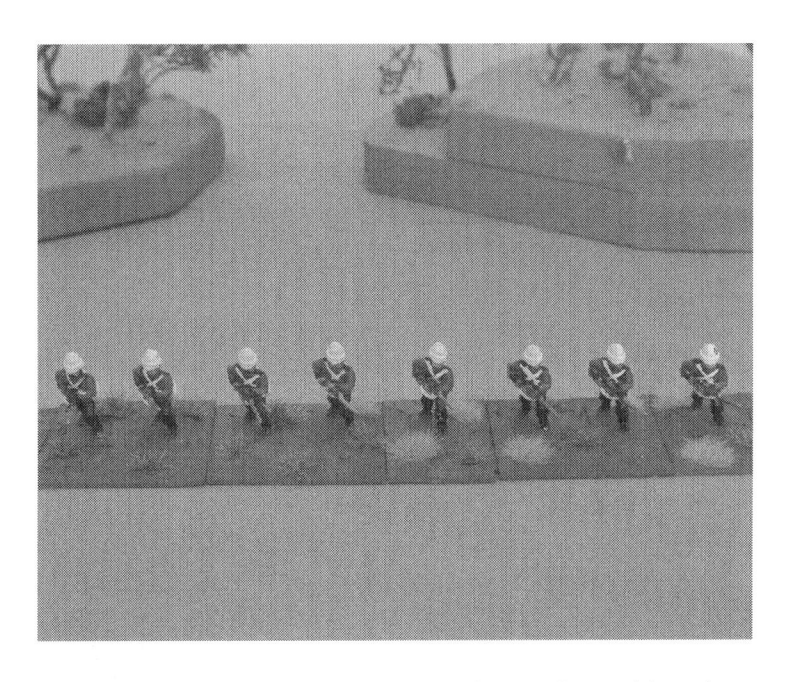

British Regular's make a bayonet charge. Something that seldom actually happened during the Zulu War but was resorted to with good effect at the battle of Khambula.

BRITISH

British Regulars is the term that I have used to describe the British army infantry as opposed to the Naval contingents of regular troops that were fielded. These are classified as Naval Brigade.

British Regulars.

A British infantry battalion comprised notionally eight companies, each of which totalled around 110 men and officers and was split into three platoons.

Each company was commanded by a Captain and there were 2 Majors and one Lieutenant Colonel for each battalion.

The battalion had additionally supporting commissariat, bandsmen, orderlies, quartermasters and so-forth. However, companies were often under-strength, so a company can safely be represented by anything from 10 to 12 figures.

Whilst the Regulars formed the backbone of the British forces in Zululand, for the sake of realism, they should not comprise more than 75% of the point value of a British force.

Naval Brigade.

Naval Brigade units may vary in size. For reference here is a note of what Naval units were involved.
HMS Tenedos fielded 61 sailors and 15 marines (wore all blue)
HMS Active fielded 196 sailors and 34 marines (wore blue with straw hats)
HMS Shah fielded 378 sailors (wore white trousers, white jumpers and blue hats)
HMS Bodicea fielded 218 sailors (wore blue jumpers, white trousers and white caps)

The Naval Brigade were noted to march/move somewhat faster than the British infantry counterparts and also to be a tad better in hand-to-hand combat where their sword bayonets undoubtedly helped them. These factors are reflected in the rules; however, to balance things out and make things realistic, a Naval Brigade element should not make up more than 25% of a British force at the very most.

Volunteer Cavalry.

Cavalry volunteer units varied mostly between 20 and 60 men and thus will be represented by typically around 4 – 8 figures. These units, such as the Buffalo Border Guard, Frontier Light Horse, etc were good horseman and good shots with their carbines but their reliability in close combat and morale was less good than the British Regulars.

Any British force should always include either some Volunteer cavalry and / or Natal Native Contingent as both were invariably used for scouting purposes.

Mounted Infantry.

Because of the shortage of cavalry, volunteers who claimed a familiarity with horses were drawn from various Regular infantry units and mounted on local horses and designated "Mounted Infantry". At the outset of hostilities around 100 Mounted Infantry were fielded under the command of Lieutenant Edward Stevenson-Brown. The men included grooms, cooks, bandsmen and privates and they were equipped with Martini-rifles. Their role was to scout on horseback and dismount to fight as infantry. They carried their ammunition in bandoliers and not pouches. They wore red jackets and whilst some wore pith helmets others might have adopted slouch hats.

In the rules they fight only fractionally less well than British Regulars but move faster because they are on horseback. However, it takes a full turn for these units to either mount up and move or dismount and prepare to fire and this is reflected in their point value.

Natal Native Contingent.

NNC were formed into companies of roughly 100 men and commanded by one European officer supported by some European and on-European NCOs. The best of the NNC were the pioneers who were even issued with old red jackets and mid-length white trousers. In the first campaign only one NNC in ten received a rifle. In the second campaign most units were disbanded but those remaining units did at least usually receive a rifle per man.

Balancing of a British force.

A British force should have a sensible balance of "red coats", Naval Brigade, cavalry, NNC and artillery.

As a guideline work with no more than one artillery unit for every 4 companies of regulars. Cavalry were always in short supply except for in the closing stages of the war, so cavalry should not make up more than around 15% of a total point value of a force. Naval Brigade should not comprise more than 25% of a force. NNC should comprise 5% - 10% of the total point value.

These figures though should be treated as guidelines. It may be that a specific wargame is to be fought that would work outside these guidelines; for example, at Holbane the British force was comprised NNC and volunteer cavalry and there were actually no British Regulars.

It will be noted that British Regulars in full-pack and therefore carrying more ammunition, come at a higher point value.

Naval Brigade.

Some had served since 1877 in South Africa and seen plenty of action. Like the British redcoats they were armed with Martini-Henry rifles but they had 1871 pattern cutlass-bayonets. Their straw hats and loose fitting uniforms were better suited to the climate and they were noted to be able to move somewhat faster that the recoats and they fought in hand-to-hand combat with distinction.

On the left of picture are Marines.

ZULUS

Zulu regiments varied in size considerably, but most regiments numbered between 500 and 2,500 warriors and each regiment was sub-divided into four or more companies, with each forming a horn, chest or loins of the regiment and each with its own officer. A Zulu brigade comprised usually four or more regiments again with each regiment assuming a role of horn, chest or loins.

For the purpose of the wargame, I'd suggest Zulu regiments should be represented by between typically 30 and 150 figures. Larger regiments should be avoided as utterly unwieldy on a wargame table.

Sometimes they fought in full-regalia but more often they fought without all the uniform adornments that made each regiment so distinctive. For wargaming purposes therefore, I have nearly all of my Zulu regiments in full uniform.

For ease of identification indunas should be based on circular bases.

When wargaming the Zulu side, the player is advised to deploy in closed rank formations when outside of the range of fire of the British and to move to engagement distance in skirmish formation. Otherwise, casualties will be crippling. Once the Zulus are at close range, they can opt to lie down whilst more move in to join them and other units move into their respective positions. Then once ready the final charge can be made in closed formation.

Terminology
Zulu Army = Impi
Zulu Regiment = Ibutho
Zulu Company = Iviyo
Zulu Commander = Induna

Zulu regiments raised pre-1850 were by the time of the Zulu War in 1879, although often supplemented with a draft of younger men, generally warriors in their fifties, sixties or even older. They did not have the stamina of younger regiments and less was expected of them. Thus, they carry only 1 point per figure. At least 20% of the Zulu force should be pre-1850 raised regiments.

Typically, around 10% - 20% of the Zulu force should be riflemen.

For these rules I have singled out the umCijo regiment as the Zulu regiment with the greatest battle honours and prowess and thus whilst they were a black shield regiment their military record throughout the war surpassed most of the other Zulu regiments and for that reason they are classified "elite" and carry a value of 3 points per figure. For wargaming purposes players may prefer to elect another regiment but this must be signalled at the outset obviously. The uMbonambi could be another worthy contender for an "elite" classification. They were alongside the umCijo the first to launch their charge against the British ranks at Islandlwana. Leaving the cover of the Mpofane donga they charged headlong at

"A" Company whom they swept backwards in a maelstrom of furious hand-to-hand combat. The uMbonambi was a very old regiment, first raised during the reign of Shaka but then re-formed in 1863 and given their performance at Isandlwana and later Kambula and Gingindlovu, it seems likely that the majority of the warriors were men in their thirties and that the older veterans in their fifties or even older were by 1879 a minority within the ranks.

For the player who is in command of the Zulus it makes sense to deploy their pre-1850 raised regiments in a supporting or secondary role and to use the younger/faster regiments to do the bulk of the work. For example, at Isandlwana, the UmKhultshane regiment comprised men who were in their fifties and sixties. The regiment kept its head down until the umCijo had rushed upon the British ranks and then they joined in the attack.

At long range Zulu advances will obviously be subjected to artillery fire and then gatling guns and thus if the Zulus can make numerous combined simultaneous attacks, it will be harder for the British to repulse these than were the Zulus to make individual/piecemeal attacks. Simply put the British artillery can only be firing in one direction at any one time.

Whilst sniper fire from the Zulus will undoubtedly inflict some casualties the only way the Zulus can ever be certain of victory is if they can engage in hand-to-hand combat, therefore they have to bring a significant number of warriors into close quarters combat. For the Zulu to close the distance upon the British without suffering appalling casualties in the early stages of the wargame, movement in skirmish order is imperative.

The Zulu player should endeavour to get at least several regiments to within charge distance before launching his final attack.

For the British to win they need to break the morale of the Zulus by inflicting heavy casualties before the Zulus can get into hand-to-hand combat. Once an impi has suffered notable casualties it will be forced to withdraw and regroup. At this juncture if the British can unleash cavalry and NNC to pursue and hound the impi, it can invariably turn a retreat into a rout.

Each Zulu regiment should have one Induna and in addition there should be an overall Commander in Chief.

In the event of the Zulu commander in chief being killed, overall command automatically passes to the Induna commanding the most senior (by shield colour/size) regiment.

For ease of identification each senior commander might be based on a circle rather than a rectangle and then identified accordingly.

THE ZULU RESERVE

Given the quantity of wargame figures needed to represent a Zulu force it is worth applying the following consideration: each Zulu army comprised a chest, horns and loin with one or several regiments forming each. There was always a reserve also. Typically, the reserve was around 20% of the total strength. Therefore, a marker can be used to indicate the location of this "Reserve" unit, and it can be activated and brought into play as soon as the Zulus have suffered casualties totalling the strength of the "Reserve".

~~

DEPLOYMENT/POINT VALUES

The following points can be used to assemble matching forces:-

Zulu regiments raised pre-1850	1
Zulu regiments raised post 1850	2
Zulu "elite" (umCijo) regiment	3
Zulu riflemen	3
Zulu Induna	5
Zulu Chief Induna	18
British Colonel	18
British Lieutenant Colonel	15
British Major/Commodore	12
British Regulars	10
Naval Brigade	12
British Regulars in full pack	14
NNC (first campaign)	1
NNC (second campaign)	2
Boers	8
Non-European volunteer mounted units	6
European volunteer units – infantry	6
European volunteer units – mounted	13
British dis/mounted infantry	8
British Regular Cavalry	20
Gatling Gun	46
Field guns 7pdr	75
Field guns 9pdr	85
Rocket launcher	25
Limber and horses	10

COMMANDERS

"We know how well carried out, tactically speaking, were the Zulu Generals' strategic arrangements. In the attack on the camp there was no hurry or excitement on their part. They first outflanked and surrounded it, and then, and not till then, did they give way to their natural impetuosity and charge with the assegai"

Charles L Norris Newman, Special Correspondent, The Zulu War.

"Bis peccare in bello non licet"
In war one may not blunder twice

British

Size of force and command requirements:-

1,000 points +: Colonel.
700 – 999 points: Lieutenant Colonel.
699 - 500 points: either a Colonel or Lieutenant Colonel.
499 points or less: either a Lieutenant Colonel or a Major.

For every 4 companies of British Regulars there must be 1 Major.

Each British company has 1 Captain: Captains are regarded as junior commanders.

A force of +1,000 points may have both a Colonel and Lieutenant Colonel, if preferred.

For ease of identification each senior commander might be based on a circle rather than a rectangle and then identified accordingly.

Naval Brigade may not exceed 25% of total points. (typically)
Only 1 artillery unit per 4 companies of British Regulars. (as a guide)
Mounted troops may not exceed 15% of total points. (as a guide)

ORDER OF PLAY

Establish how many points each side is to have, how scenery should be arranged and what the purpose of the game is.

Generally speaking, the Zulus should have the option of coming onto the battlefield from either one, two or three sides and the British only have the option of entering the stage from the one remaining side.

Lay out the scenery first and agree an objective. Next agree the direction from which the British are advancing. Both sides should then deploy. Obviously concealed Zulu forces must be deployed beyond the range at which they become visible. Some degree of common sense and mutual agreement has to prevail during deployment.

If the British are pre-deployed in a defensive position such as a hilltop, then they should only be allowed two-thirds or half the point value attributed to the Zulus. And if the British are in a defensive position affording mostly hard-cover, such as a Rorke's Drift type location, then their point value should be even less.

Both sides move simultaneously and moving is conducted first, then firing and finally hand to hand combat.

The Zulus, to stand any chance of winning, must obviously get into hand-to-hand combat. For the British to be assured a victory they need to try to avoid the Zulus getting the bulk of their force into hand-to-hand combat.

The British need to make every effort to scout well or they will be ambushed. The British commander also needs to be mindful of ammunition consumption. Once firing, keep a count of how many rounds of ammunition are expended!

Written orders should be put on unit control sheets and these should state the units name, number of troops, etc and should have a simple turn/column layout so for each turn the player simply fills under "move" a yes or a no and likewise for whether the units fires and there should be a column to record the casualties the unit takes each turn.

MOVEMENT

	Large Table inches	Small Table
centimetres		
Zulus (regiments raised pre- 1850)	8"	15cm
Zulus (regiments raised post- 1850)	10"	18cm
Natal Native Contingent	6"	10cm
Boers	6"	10cm
Non-European Volunteers (Infantry)	6"	10cm
Non-European Volunteer (Mounted)	9"	15cm
European Volunteer Infantry	5"	9cm
European Volunteer Cavalry	9"	15cm
British Regulars	4"	8cm
Naval Brigade	5"	10cm
Mounted Infantry *	6"	10cm
British Regular Cavalry	6"	12cm
Field guns limbered	5"	8cm
Field guns un-limbered	2"	3cm
Gatling guns limbered	6"	9cm
Gatling guns un-limbered	2"	3cm
Rocket launchers; man handled	4"	8cm
CHARGE: Zulus	+4"	+6cm.
British infantry	+2"	+4cm
Boers/ NNC	+3"	+5cm
Cavalry	+6" +	10cm.

MOVEMENT

Cavalry take 1 turn to halt and about face; half a turn to wheel, dismount or mount.

British units can make a half move and go from skirmish to closed order or visa-versa in 1 turn.
Infantry retreating whilst still facing the enemy deduct 50% from their move distance.

A charge may only be implemented to engage an enemy. It may also only be implemented 1 turn in every 10. An infantry charge lasts 1 turn a cavalry charge 2 turns. Cavalry must canter before making a charge.

Cavalry may elect to canter which gives them +3" or +6cm but on the following turn they must then either return to trot/walk or progress to "charge". Cavalry may canter every other turn.

*Mounted Infantry moved as cavalry but always fought as infantry. To obviate the cost to the Wargamer of providing these men with horses, or having two actual sets of figures, one mounted and one dismounted, it can be taken that they move on horseback but are dismounted when fighting and only one set of dismounted figures need be used. Being drawn from the "odds & ends" of the line companies dismounted infantry fight and fire slightly less well than British Regulars. Whilst they may canter, they are not allowed to charge. It takes one full turn for Mounted Infantry to dismount and prepare lines to fire and it takes one full turn for them to cease firing and re-mount and turn to move off. For the avoidance of doubt

"Mounted Infantry" and "Dismounted Infantry" are one and the same but for accuracy they might be called the former when moving and the latter when fighting.

British troops in combat dress carry 40 rounds. If wearing full pack, they have 70 rounds.

Artillery requires a full turn to unlimber and prepare to fire.

Troops moving in skirmish order, taking advantage of what cover there is and making an effort to avoid being bunched up and present an easier target to the enemy are going to take markedly less casualties from rifle fire etc. However, to qualify as being in skirmish order, the bases of units must be more than a base distance apart from each other.

A further British option, to closed ranks or skirmish order, is "open" order. Movement speed is normal, and bases are again spaced apart but at 50% further than the space of closed order. The moving troops must form a line. British troops in "open" order are slightly less vulnerable to enemy rifle fire but will be disadvantaged when in hand-to-hand combat because the Zulus can pour through such a thinly spread deployment line.

TERRAIN PENALTIES

Hill contours represented by a 1" (approx) rise, imply an assent of 450 feet.
Moving through soft cover -25%
Moving up hill -33% per contour
Moving down hill + 25% per contour
Small rivers take 1 full turn for cavalry to cross and 2 full turns for infantry to cross.
Artillery and gatling guns cannot be moved up/down hill except when limbered.
Contours that are closer together than 3" cannot be negotiated by artillery whether limbered or unlimbered.
Contours closer together than 2" preclude cavalry from charging up or down hill.
Contours that are closer together than 1" cannot be negotiated by cavalry unless they dismount and cannot be negotiated by British Regulars in full pack.

CONCEALMENT

Zulus may deploy concealed forces which must be shown by a paper flag/marker with an identifying code. The British will be aware of some enemy in this position, but the strength of the unit will not be apparent until troops advance to within 12" or 20cm. The concealed Zulus may then be properly identified and fired upon. Concealment markers must be spaced suitably apart. A concealed forces marker may be in scrub, heavy undergrowth, dongas, or behind hill/s and can represent a force of any size, so long as that force can realistically be hidden in that position. For example, a stand of a few trees and a couple of bushes could conceal a few skirmishers but there is no way an impi of a thousand warriors could be hidden there. However, a very large hill could easily conceal the latter.

Concealment and a successful surprise attack is the Zulu ace card. At the battle of Inyezane, a modestly sized Zulu Impi of 6,000 warriors attempted an ambush of No.1. Column under Pearson. Pearson had around 2,400 men with artillery and was marching in column. An NNC company sent to clear a handful of Zulus from some ground ahead prematurely sprung a Zulu trap. Hundreds of Zulu sprang from the undergrowth and whilst the NNC rank and file legged it, their European officers just about had time to say; "I say you chaps, stand firm!" before they were engulfed by a tidal wave of Zulu warriors. However, the rest of the British got enough warning of the ambush to sort themselves out and they won the day.

However, Inyezane could nearly have turned into a disaster for the British who had nearly blundered into a well laid ambush. The much-derided NNC had on this occasion saved the day!

The Zulus may deploy up to 50% of the force as "concealed" and can elect to deploy visible troops closer to the British or further away, depending on the terrain and what suits their tactics.

Dongas, scrub and hills will all provide opportunity for Zulus to conceal forces and it is British best practice to scout these with cavalry, NNC or mounted infantry. The British player should however be mindful that whilst these units have good mobility, they are not well placed to engage in hand-to-hand combat against strong Zulu forces and it was common practice for them to be beefed-up with some Company Regulars when entering upon skirmish fighting against defended positions.

ZULU RESERVE UNITS OFF TABLE

The Zulu player may choose to keep up to 20% of his forces off the table at the outset and brought on during the first six turns. However, the units chosen for this must be written down / mapped accordingly and specifically which sector of the table they wish to come on from and specifically upon which turn. This must be decided before the wargame starts and cannot be altered afterwards.

Unless there is scenery blocking the British view, the British will see these units 3 turns before they come into play and the Zulu player must notify the British commander accordingly.

For example, the Zulu player is starting the game deploying his force on the west, north and east sides of the wargame table. He has 8 impis totalling 8,000 warriors. He could issue written orders to say that the iKhwentu impi numbering 700 warriors is to come into play on the southern end of the eastern side of the wargame table on turn 6 and that the umXhapo impi numbering 1,100 warriors is to come into play from the central western side of the table on turn 8. On turn 2 the Zulu player notifies the British player about the iKhwentu. The British player may elect to move more troops to cover this threat and will remain unaware of the additional threat coming from the opposite side by the umXhapo until the beginning of turn 5.

FIREPOWER

Use 2 six-sided dice

Firing

To hit enemy at long range, requires a dice score of 10 – 12
To hit enemy at medium range, requires a dice roll of 9 – 12
To hit enemy at short range, requires a dice roll of 8 – 12

Modifiers:-

Troops under fire are in skirmish order – 2 from dice roll
Troops under fire are in "open" order -1 from dice roll
Troops under fire are kneeling -1 from dice roll
Troops under fire are lying down – 2 from dice roll
Troops under fire are behind soft cover -1 from dice roll
Troops under fire are behind hard cover – 2 from dice roll
Unit firing are Natal Native Mounted Contingent -1 from dice roll.
Unit firing are NNC – 2 from dice roll
Unit firing are Zulus – 2 from dice roll.
British use "quick fire" + 1 to dice roll
British use "independent fire" +2 to dice roll.

The maximum accrued bonus allowed is 4. Thus, troops lying down, behind hard cover and in skirmish order would still only be awarded a -4 benefit.

Example: a company of British Regulars fire at Zulus in skirmish order at medium range. The British need a dice roll of 9 for each man firing modified by -2, so a dice roll of 11 or 12 will be needed to hit. The two dice are rolled for each man firing, so they are rolled 10 times. On 2 occasions a roll of 11 or higher is achieved, so the Zulus take 2 casualties.

Zulus and NNC cannot fire at "quick" or "independent" fire rates.

British Regulars cannot kneel unless they are under fire and have taken casualties. They can only lie down after they have taken casualties on two successive turns. The British were very loath to do anything but "stand firm" and face the fire of enemy irregulars until it became too deadly. It was not until the 1st Boer War and the Sudan campaign that the galling fire from the enemy brought about a realisation that standing in neat lines was not the best of ideas.

It will be noted from the above that at long range the Zulus can only inflict casualties on the British if they are lucky enough to roll a 12.

British Regulars can move and fire with a half move distance and a single volley fire, one round only at a -1 modifier.

European Volunteer units including cavalry may do the same with the same modifier.

Zulus and NNC cannot move and fire in the same turn.

FIRING

The Martini-Henry was sighted up to 1,450 yards but was very seldom fired at such extreme range. 7pdr artillery fired up to 3,100 yards, the 9pdr had a shorter range but a bigger shell. Rockets could fire up to 1,300 yards and gatling guns up to 1,200 yards.

Firing should be conducted by unit; ie: 1 British Regular Company. However, it is allowed for a unit to split its fire against 2 enemy units, even at different ranges but both must parts of the Company must fire at the same rate of fire.

Firing is conducted after movement.

British Regulars / Naval Brigade can move and volley-fire with a half movement rate and a single volley firing one round only and at a -1 modifier. Regular and Volunteer European cavalry may do the same.

Zulus and NNC cannot move and fire in the same turn.

If a unit of Zulus is moving to attack a British unit and gets into hand-to-hand combat, then the British unit is still able to fire at them but given the following provisos:

The distance covered in the turn is below 4" or 7cm the firing unit may only fire a single 1 round volley.

The distance covered is between 4" or 7cm and 8" or 15cm the firing unit may fire at "steady" rate.

The distance is above 8" or 15cm the firing unit may fire at "quick fire" rate.

The defending unit may not fire at "independent" fire rate.

Remember to record all ammunition expenditure. The British player should try not to expend too much ammunition firing at targets that are either at long range or in skirmish order.

A British player with nerves of steel may even have his troops not fire their first volley until the Zulus are at medium range!

Firing Range Large tabletop using inches

	Short range	Medium range	Long range
Martini Henry	-15"	15" – 21"	22" – 30"
Carbine	-10"	10" – 17"	18" – 22"
Gatling gun			28"
Rocket			30"
7pdr field gun			36"
9pdr field gun3			32"

Firing Range Small tabletop using centimetres

	Short range	Medium range	Long range
Martini Henry	-20cm	21cm – 34cm	35cm – 55cm
Carbine	-18cm	19cm – 31cm	32cm – 40cm
Gatling gun	-20cm	20cm – 49cm	50cm
Rocket			50cm
7pdr field gun			70cm
9pdr field gun			60cm

EXPENDITURE OF AMMUNITION

British troops carry 70 rounds if wearing full pack. If in battle dress they carry only 40 rounds.

Expended ammunition must be noted based upon the following rates of fire.
- "Steady Fire" rate.   = 2 rounds per turn
- "Quick Fire" rate.   = 4 rounds per turn
- "Independent Fire"   = 5 rounds per turn

Each British unit must record its ammunition expenditure per turn as it will be noted that the impetuous use of ammunition could result in a unit running out of ammunition within as little as eight turns. Mounted Infantry carry 40 rounds in bandolier format and carried rifles not carbines.

Zulus carry 40 rounds and can only fire at a rate of 2 rounds "steady" per turn.

NNC carry 10 rounds and can only fire at a rate of 2 rounds "steady" per turn.

GATLING GUNS

There is a 1 in 6 chance per turn that a gatling gun will jam after it has fired for more than one turn. In other words, on its 2nd turn firing if it rolls a 1 then it has jammed.

If a gatling gun jams, then it will inflict only 1 casualty in that turn and the remainder of the turn is spent clearing the jam so that it can start afresh on the following turn.

A gatling gun will inflict 3 casualties at close range, 2 at medium range and 1 casualty at long range. If the enemy are in skirmish order or lying down casualties at medium are allowed a saving throw of a 6 and at long range, they are allowed a saving throw of a 5, 6.

ROCKETS

These are notoriously inaccurate. Pre-set fuses determine range but this can vary and rockets can veer off course. If a rocket is being fired at a large body of enemy it has a better chance of at least landing in amongst them.

Roll 1 six sided dice and adjust score as follows:-

- − 2 for enemy unit contains less than 15 figures
- − 1 for enemy unit contains 16 – 35 figures
- − 1 for enemy in skirmish order
- − 1 for enemy in cover
- + 1 for enemy unit above 50 figures
- + 1 if the rocket unit has not moved this turn.

Adjusted dice roll

1 no casualties
2 no casualties
3 1 dead
4 1 dead
5 2 dead
6 2 dead

Example: a dice roll of 4 against a unit of 60 Zulus will inflict 2 casualties.

Rockets were not that cumbersome to carry, set up and fire, so it is possible to move and fire in the same turn or to fire with an advantage if the battery hasn't moved. It should be considered that a rocket unit carries enough rockets to fire 15 turns.

While Rockets are clearly less formidable than artillery, they are very portable and cost the British player few points.

ARTILLERY

7pdr maximum range	36"	70cm
9pdr maximum range	32"	60cm

It should be considered that artillery carry enough rounds to fire for 12 turns.

Roll 1 six-sided dice to determine enemy casualties.

- 1   1 dead
- 2   1 dead
- 3   1 dead
- 4   2 dead
- 5   2 dead
- 6   3 dead

+1   for enemy in closed order & 3 or more ranks deep
+1   for enemy closer than 18" or 32cm
+1   for 9pdr firing
-1   for enemy lying down
-1   for enemy in skirmish order

Example: a 9pdr guns fires at closer than 32cm at a unit of Zulus who are 3 ranks deep. The dice roll is a "3" and the score is modified by 3 = 4 Zulu casualties.

Example: a 7pdr gun fires at long range into a unit of Zulus in skirmish order. The dice roll is "3" and the score modifier is -1, so there are no Zulu casualties.

If artillery are caught into hand-to-hand combat they fight as "Dismounted Mounted" and carry the same point value per figure.

While artillery can be moved by limber, for most wargames it is likely that they will remain in one place throughout the wargame, so the British player needs to give careful consideration to their position and that they are not placed where they are likely to overrun by the Zulus or forced to move.

British Infantry Unit Commanders

Role a dice before the start of the game to determine the character of each unit commander. Dice roll of 1 is a "cautious" commander and a dice roll of "6" is an "impetuous" commander.

Cautious infantry commanders will never allow independent fire unless a senior officer is attached to them.

Impetuous infantry commanders will never fire at "steady" rate unless a senior commander is attached to them.

Unit Commanders amongst the casualties

Casualties should be assigned randomly but if the figure that is to be removed is the "officer" figure then it is considered that the officer is indeed amongst the casualties.
In such a case, with the loss of say a Captain, a Lieutenant will assume command of a company.

Commander casualties become more significant when Zulu Indunas are killed or where British officers of Major or above are killed and the effect of this is noted under "morale."

British officers being made of stern stuff and possessing a stiff upper lip, were happy to expose themselves to danger and frequently stood in the front line. However, Zulu Indunas invariably showed great wisdom and would let lieutenants lead from the front whilst the Induna commanded from atop a nice hill, from where he could watch what was happening and direct his troops accordingly.

HAND TO HAND COMBAT

All figures in base-to-base contact are considered in hand-to-hand combat. If figures are facing away from an enemy, then they may not fight those figures who are behind them if they are also figures fighting in front of them. If they are only fighting figures behind them, they may fight at half unit strength.

Figures in hand-to-hand combat point value

- British regulars   8
- Naval Brigade   10
- British dis/mounted infantry   6
- Zulus pre-1850   4
- Zulus post-1850   5
- UmCijo "Elite"   6
- British regular cavalry   10
- British lancer cavalry   11
- Volunteer European cavalry   8
- Volunteer Native cavalry   5
- Boers   5
- NNC   4

The point value of a figure represents the number on 2 dice that the figure needs to roll or to roll below to make their saving throw.

Example: 10 Naval Brigade are in hand-to-hand combat with 10 Zulus of a post-1850 regiment. Each Naval Brigade must roll a 10 or below to "save". Each Zulu must roll a 5 or below. So, the British player rolls the dice

10 times in his defence and each time he rolls an 11 or a 12 then he removes one Naval Brigade figure. The Zulu player rolls the dice 10 times and each time he fails to roll 5 or below he removes 1 Zulu figure.

If troops are being attacked from behind, then they deduct 1 from their saving throw.

Troops that are charged by a unit in closed formation deduct 1 from their saving throw for one turn.

Troops that are defending a hill add 1 to their saving throw for the first turn of combat.

Troops that are defending a redoubt or similar can add 1 to their saving throw for every turn of combat.

It is obviously dangerous for a British unit, whether cavalry or infantry to have its flank/s enveloped by the enemy as it will mean that the Zulus can add more men into the fray. Worst still is for the Zulus to be allowed to attack the British from behind as well. Once this happens a Company of British regulars is all but doomed. If the British commander sees the potential for this to happen, he should endeavour to form Company square as fast as possible. Ideally Companies of British regulars should keep their flanks protected by a neighbouring unit.
If the British are in danger of being completely surrounded by Zulus, then the British commander may elect to bring his whole force into a large "Regimental" size square. The advantage of this is obvious in terms of defence however the disadvantage is it means that the force is inevitably encircled, loses the opportunity to

manoeuvre and will probably be subjected to Zulu sniper fire whilst the Zulus edge forwards all of their forces before finally launching an all-out attack.

The Senior Commanders bonus

The hand-to-hand combat point value of a unit of British troops may be raised by 1 if the unit is led by a Major, Commodore, Lieutenant Colonel or Colonel but the officer must be in the ranks of fighting troops and not behind. Likewise, for a Zulu Impi led by their Induna.

The senior commander must be, if British, in the front rank alongside the men and if Zulu, must be in one of the front two ranks of an Impi. If the senior commander is killed the bonus is immediately lost. Additionally, there may be a morale issue.

"The Colours"

The Zulu War was one of the last campaigns where the British took their Regimental colours onto the field of battle. Alongside the Regimental colours there was of course the Union Flag.

British forces of over 700 points or more may opt to have a standard bearer with "The Colours" and this of course should be placed on the battlefield alongside the Commander in chief, be he Colonel or Lieutenant Colonel.

If the Zulu player is able to take "The Colours" then, unless they are recaptured by the British in the next turn, the wargame is a Zulu victory.

Morale Check for Zulus:-

A Zulu Ibutho must be under fire for a morale check to be made and the impi must have taken casualties as follows:

Impi of under 39 figures	6 casualties or more
Impi of 40 – 59 figures	8 casualties or more
Impi of 60 – 79 figures	10 casualties of more
Impi of 80 – 100 figures	15 casualties or more
Impi of 101+ figures	20 casualties or more

If the Ibutho has not got into hand-to-hand combat and has taken casualties as noted above, then it may only continue to advance as long as it is within sight of another impi which is still also seen to be advancing and that impi is closer to the enemy than the impi under morale test.

If the Ibutho has not got into hand-to-hand combat and has taken more than twice the casualties noted above, then it may only continue to advance if another Zulu impi has already got into hand-to-hand combat. Otherwise, it will lie down and wait for another Ibutho to get into hand-to-hand to combat first before resuming its advance.

If a Zulu Ibutho has taken twice the casualties as noted above but has got into hand-to-hand combat it can continue to fight unless the impi has taken more than 3 times the above casualty rate, in which see next condition…

If a Zulu Ibutho has got into hand-to-hand combat and is the only Ibutho in hand-to-hand combat and suffers more than three times the casualties noted above, then the Ibutho must retreat in skirmish order until it is out of enemy firing range. At that point, if the unit is not under pursuit, it will rally, if the majority of the Zulu Ibuthos in battle are still fighting and/or not in retreat and the Ibutho commander has not been killed.

If a Zulu Ibutho has got into hand-to-hand combat it will continue to fight even with over 3 times the casualties as long as there are at least two other Zulu Ibutho in hand-to-hand combat as well.

Once a Zulu Impi collectively has sustained 25% casualties, if it has not got in any way into hand-to-hand combat, then it will break off the engagement and retreat in good order. If this happens and the British fail to turn the retreat into a rout then the wargame is a draw.

If a Zulu Impi has got into hand-to-hand combat it will continue to fight until it sustains in 33% casualties. At that point it will continue to fight so long as over 50% of the British force has been destroyed. If the British have sustained less than 50% casualties then the Zulus will break off the engagement and retreat in good order. This outcome is classed as draw.

Morale Check for British forces:-

- NNC units will "retreat" in order when faced by Zulus unless they outnumber in points the Zulus or unless a friendly force is closer to them than the Zulus. The friendly force must be at least 50% of the strength of the NNC unit.
- NNC units will "rout" when charged by a Zulu force that exceeds their strength unless they are directly supported by another friendly unit.
- NNC units with over 50% casualties will rout unless contained and supported within the framework of a Batallion square.
- European Volunteer and non-European Volunteers will always "retreat" when faced by any Zulu force that is at least their size or larger, unless the unit is supported by a unit of British Regulars that is the same strength or greater than the volunteer unit. However mounted units may fire and retreat, effectively falling back in a controlled and orderly fashion until the can be supported by other friendly units.
- Any Volunteer unit that suffers 50% casualties in hand-to-hand combat with Zulus will "rout" unless there is a British Major or higher rank attached or adjacent to this unit.
- Any British regular unit that suffers over 33% casualties may not move and must attempt to form company square if engaged in hand-to-hand combat with Zulus unless it is supported by a

Major or senior officer in which case it can elect to adopt any formation or movement option.
- Any British regular unit that suffers over 50% casualties and is in hand-to-hand combat must attempt to form company square unless it is already part of a Battalion square.
- If a British force loses all senior commanders of rank Major and higher and has taken collectively 50%+ casualties, then it must attempt to retreat away from the enemy. All units will fire at independent fire until their ammunition is exhausted. All non-regular units, ie: NNC, Volunteers, etc, will rout. If the force is surrounded and unable retreat, then it will fight in square until the last man falls. In this scenario the battle is declared a Zulu victory.

Deployment to battalion or regimental square

A Major must be accompanying any force larger than a single Company which wishes to form a square combining the separate units up to the size of 4 Companies. To form a square larger than 4 Companies but no larger than 8 Companies requires either 2 Majors or a Major plus a Lieutenant Colonel or Colonel.

There must be a commanding officer rank of Lieutenant Colonel or Colonel present for a British force of larger than 8 Companies to for a square.

For the purpose of forming a Battalion or Regimental size square, a "Company" in counting Companies must include all units that are to participate either in forming the Square or being within the protection of the Square.

For example, a British force of 5 Companies of Regulars, 1 Company of Naval Brigade, 1 unit of artillery and 2 Companies of NNC would total 9 Companies and therefore require the command of a Lieutenant Colonel or Colonel.

The Battle of Zwingdulanye – a wargame

The following is a brief summary of a test wargame for the rules played out recently.

The British player fielded a 1,500 point force comprising 2 Companies 91st Highlanders, 2 Companies 80th Regiment, Staffordshire Volunteers, Naval Brigade detachments from HMS Active, 120 men and HMS Bodicea, 88 men, 56 Mounted Infantry, 72 cavalry of 17th Lancers, 40 Frontier Light Horse, 40 Natal Mounted Carbineers, artillery of the Royal Horse and HMS Active, a gatling gun, a rocket launcher and 2 Companies NNC. All under the command of a Colonel with a Lieutenant Colonel, a Commodore and a Major in addition.

The Zulu player fielded a 1,500 point force comprising 10 Ibutho, (regiments) totalling 7,000 warriors. Four of the ten Ibutho were raised pre-1850, and of the other six, one was the elite umCijo. Three of the Ibutho included riflemen, so of the 7,000 warriors, 500 were rifle armed.

The British made an advance from the south side of the wargame table, the Zulu lay awaiting them to the north. The terrain was a mix of hills, dongas, scrubland and open plain.

British scouts gave ample warning of the Zulu Impi to the north of the British advance, so the British deployed to fight with units deploying not just to face north but to face west and east as well. The British were able to occupy two small hills on their west flank and deployed the remainder of their force in fairly open ground facing north and east.

The Zulu commander opened the battle with a heavy but basically ineffectual barrage of sniper fire from a long distance and for the Zulus from the relative safety of thick undergrowth and dongas. At the same time, two Zulu Ibutho raced as the horns of the Buffalo to encircle the British flanks.

A ruined farmhouse midway between both sides was seized by the British with a unit of NNC and tentative Zulu advances against this were deterred by a show of the 17th Lancers. The British opened fire on all sides as the Zulus began to advance.

By turn 9 three of the Zulu Ibutho were pinned down by heavy fire, including the inGobamakhosi and the inNdluyengwe who formed the horns of the attack and on the western flank the black shield uMbonambi. The Zulus were taking appalling casualties. The British losses were thus far light, and the British player was sensing victory.

In turn 10 the inDlondlo, though badly mauled by heavy fire, managed to get into hand-to-hand combat against the north-east corner of the British positions which was held by "D" Company of the 80th. Seeing this the Zulu commander unleashed the last units he had held back in reserve. The elite umCijo and the isAnagqu moved rapidly against the British north and east facing lines.

In turn 11 the white shield uThulwana charged the NNC defending the ruined farmhouse. The 17th lancers again moved to break this charge but were in turn charged in their flank by elements of the uMbonambi. Wheeling to meet this threat the Lancers were then flank charged by some of the uThulwana whilst others over-ran the ruined farmhouse which the NNC abandoned. Although "D" Company 80th Regiment in closed ranks with bayonets were holding back the inDlondlo a small regiment of grizzled olders the umKultshane were moving to join the fight.

The NNC joined the British lines forming up between the hill held by the 90th and the Naval Brigade who formed the north line of the British defence. The 17th Lancers to avoid being trapped between the uThulwana and uMbonami cut their way clear and galloped back to the main British positions. With the retreating Lancers compromising the British field of fire the umCijo and uThulwana raced ever closer.

In turn 12 the inDlondlo and umKultshane broke through "D" Company 80th and at the same time the umCijo and uThulwana closed on the British north line of defence. The NNC with the mounted Lancers standing firing their carbines over the heads of the NNC and supported by a field gun and oblique fire from the British Regulars was, even combined, not enough fire to stop the Zulu charge reaching the British lines. The British north line collapsed. The Naval Brigade were in time to form a company square, and the Zulu tidal wave surged around them. "D" Company 80th, the NNC, the Lancers and artillery were swept away, and the Zulus poured between the British on the hills facing west and the other British units facing east.

The British commander was able to reform all the units on the west into a defensive formation centred on the two hills but the half of his force to the east was encircled and cut to pieces. Subsequent Zulu attempts to overrun the British on the hills were repulsed. The Zulu commander decided his force had done enough and he withdrew. The badly mauled British had been lucky to survive. Whilst the Zulus casualties were appallingly high the British had been even higher, and the British player conceded that victory should go to the Zulu player.

A suggested wargame.

None of the British crossings of the river border between Zululand and British Natal were contested by the Zulu and each makes for an interesting wargame scenario. Centre column crossed the Buffalo river near Rorke's Drift. A pont and a raft (made from casks and timber to RE design) were used to ferry the Regulars across platoon at a time. Both were hawser operated. There was also a small rowing boat which could take fifteen or so passengers at a time. The NNC crossed a little way upstream where the river was waist high. The cavalry crossed a way apart, fording the river at the actual drift where there were flat rocks in the riverbed at the old traders crossing point. The crossing was covered by the artillery from the west bank. This scenario of a British river crossing contested by a Zulu force would certainly make for an interesting engagement.

Conclusion

The Zulu War presents an opportunity for a highly colourful wargame between two very contrasting opponents. The battles that were fought show that whilst there was a certain sense of an inevitable British victory to the war, the Zulu army was certainly capable of inflicting a defeat upon the British given an opportunity to unleash a surprise attack or a well-co-ordinated attack using the classical fighting bull buffalo tactics.

There were essentially nine notable engagements. The first battle at Holbane was a series of running skirmishes inconclusive for both sides. Inyezane was a British win but the British were very nearly caught completely by surprise while badly deployed, so they were very lucky. Isandlwana was a decisive Zulu victory. Rorke's Drift was a British win. Ntombe Drift was a Zulu win. The second battle of Holbane was a Zulu win. Then the last three battles of the war were all won by the British.

Surprise was undoubtedly a key factor for a Zulu success and whilst the British may have enjoyed the advantage afforded by the modern firepower, the Zulus could easily out manoeuvre the British so ultimately anything could happen!

From a wargaming point of view the British player needs to be ever mindful of good scouting and to keep his force prepared for an attack in every direction.

For the Zulu player victory can come from launching a series of well-coordinated and determined attacks, especially if the Zulus can catch the British in a poorly deployed position.

The Zulu player may be tempted to rush units into hand-to-hand combat piecemeal, but they should be mindful that, time is actually on their side. Gradually encircling the British, the Zulu commander can probe for weaknesses, provoke the British player into ammunition expenditure and use his riflemen to edge closer and to stress the British with continuing sniper fire.

Keep in mind that even at a steady rate of fire, British Regulars in battle dress will run out ammunition in 20 turns and if units continually fire at independent fire this is reduced to just 8 turns!

For the British player, an impetuous Zulu massed charge against well formed ranks of Regulars is the desired thing. Just as long as the Zulus don't manage to get into hand-to-hand combat.

Even fielding large armies of 1,000 to 2,000 points it should be possible using these rules to complete a wargame in one full day. The challenge for the wargamer though wishing to battle on such a scale, is not time but it is having enough space for a suitably large wargame table.

Happy wargaming!

Bibliography

The Zulu War, Michael Barthorp, Blandford Press 1980

The War Correspondents The Anglo-Zulu War, John Laband & Ian Knight, Bramley Books, 1997

Forgotten Battles of the Zulu War, Adrian Greaves, Pen & Sword, 2012

Essential Histories The Zulu War 1879, Ian Knight, Osprey, 2003

The Zulu War, Angus McBride, Osprey, 1976

Zulu War – Volunteers, Irregulars & Auxiliaries, Ian Castle, Osprey 2003

Campaigning In Zululand, W E Montague, Leonaur, 2006

The Curling Letters of the Zulu War, edited by Adrian Greaves & Brian West, Pen & Sword, 2004

The Zulu War, David Clammer, Pan Books, 1975

In Zululand with the British Army, Charles L Norris-Newman, Leonaur, 2006

The Washing of the Spears, Donald Morris, Jonathan Cape, 1966

The Scramble for Africa, Thomas Packenham, George Weidenfeld & Nicolson, 1991

The Wedding Feast War, Keith Smith, Frontline Books, 2012

How Can Man Die Better, Lieutenant Colonel Mike Snook, Greenhill Books, 2005.

~~

Printed in Great Britain
by Amazon